BLOOD FEUD

The feud had been a long one, and had pretty well wiped out the men of the Jardin and Carter families, and the new heads, Sam Carter and Ben Jardin, were ready to end it. Sam suggested the two families show their solidarity by demanding a toll from the Texan drovers, but Ben had his doubts about the plan. However, somebody was around who didn't like the scheme at all, and when a bullet from the night cut Sam Carter down, the feud began all over again. Stopping it a second time would lead to bloodshed and death ...

BLOOD FEUD

by
Bill Wade

Dales Large Print Books
Long Preston, North Yorkshire,
England.

British Library Cataloguing in Publication Data.

Wade, Bill
  Blood feud.

  A catalogue record for this book is
  available from the British Library

  ISBN 1-85389-849-X pbk

First published in Great Britain by Robert Hale Ltd., 1993

Copyright © 1993 by Bill Wade

Cover illustration © Prieto by arrangement with Norma Editorial S.A.

The right of Bill Wade to be identified as the author of this work has been asserted by him in accordance with the Copyright, Designs and Patents Act, 1988

Published in Large Print 1998 by arrangement with Robert Hale Ltd.

Dales Large Print is an imprint of
Library Magna Books Ltd.
Printed and bound in Great Britain by
T.J. International Ltd., Cornwall, PL28 8RW.

ONE

Ben Jardin could feel the muscles of his nape and back tensing up. There was somebody out there in the night. They were watching him from well outside the sullen ring of light laid down on the riverside earth by his campfire. He was pretty sure that he knew who it was, and equally confident that they didn't mean him any harm, but he couldn't be entirely certain of that and stepped back into the darkness under the jackpines to his rear. Now, a hand upon his holster, he hopped quickly to his left—just in case—and, listening again through the night wind and the faint stirring of the foliage above him, called in a firm but friendly voice: 'I know you're there. Come on in if that's your aim. There's fresh coffee in the pot, and a mess of trout in the frying pan.'

There was a perceptible pause, then a gruff male voice said a trifle tentatively: 'That is Ben Jardin?'

Yes, the voice was familiar. Not overly so, but familiar enough. 'Sam Carter?'

'Aye.'

'You heard me, Sam. The invitation stands. You're welcome.'

Footfalls sounded at the more distant edge of the waterside clearing. They came crunching towards the fire across pebbles and driftwood—a carpet of debris probably cast up when the river had flooded during last summer's big storms in this part of northern Oklahoma—and then their maker, a huge and rather anthropoidal figure, loomed in the firelight as Jardin returned from the shadow of the jackpines. 'Well, now, Sam,' he encouraged. 'Sit yourself down. How are things back in the valley?'

'I thought it was you, Ben,' Sam Carter said, sinking down onto his backside in the brightest of the firelight's glow. 'Couldn't be sure, that's all. The trail runs back aways.'

'Sure does,' Jardin agreed inconsequentially. 'You were right to take your time. Can be dangerous to hurry these things.'

'It sure can,' Carter acknowledged wryly, 'when you're visitin' a man who's as good with a gun as I know you to be.'

'I pass,' Jardin conceded. 'You're not half bad yourself. And there's always a bit of luck in it.' Turning his head aside, he squirted a few drops of saliva through his teeth. 'But that has no place here. You said in your letter you'd ride out to meet me if you could.'

'So you got my letter okay?'

'I wouldn't be here now if I hadn't, would I?'

Carter chuckled mirthlessly. 'I guess not.'

'So how are things in Buffalo Valley?' Jordan prompted.

'Much as usual.' Carter responded. 'The members of our families are still ready to shoot each other at the smallest excuse.'

'Blasted silly feud!' Jardin sniffed. 'The crazy traditions men harness themselves to!

They're an addlepated lot over yonder in Tennessee! Who cares who pulled up that consarned root of potatoes? My grandad was worse than yours! Neither of the old fools knew who planted that tatie anyway!'

'Yeah,' Carter laughed. 'Weren't we raised on some truck, boy!'

'Twelve men have died over it across the years,' Jardin sighed. 'We've damn nigh wiped out each other's families—and for what? Honour?'

'So they say.'

'It's just a word, Sam, and the rest's pride.'

'I ain't against pride,' Carter said. 'It keeps a man against his own foolishness in some ways. But feudin' is the wrong sort. Let 'em keep it in Tennessee, I say. I always have seen myself as a Kansas man.'

'Well, you and me are now the senior men in our families since your pa went home last year,' Jardin reflected, 'and I got the impression from your writing you want to end the feud.'

'I do. That's what I'm here to talk to you about.'

'Figures.'

'What do you say, Ben?'

Jardin thrust his right hand forward and down. 'That's what I say.'

Carter's hand came up and joined Jardin's. They shook firmly.

'That accounts for us,' Jardin said. 'We'll just have to pray our doggone families follow suit.'

'I'll ride my lot hard.'

'And I'll do likewise, Sam.'

'Neither man can do more than that,' Carter said, relaxing—his big, prematurely seamed face revealed in all its pleasant ugliness by a flare up in the fire. 'Bein' head of the family ain't all it's cracked up to be. My folk take about as much notice of me as they do the old dawg. Less, maybe, of a Saturday night, when whisky's in and wit is out.'

'Oh, you've found that out, eh?' Jardin drawled humorously. 'My lot are just the same. Folk very much lead their own lives—except when they want somebody to make a difficult decision and take the responsibility.'

'We've made a difficult decision,' Carter averred, watching as the man at the other side of the campfire rummaged among the utensils spilling from a saddlebag and picked up a tin mug—'and I guess we shall have to take the responsibility too.'

'Coffee?' Jardin asked, nodding absently. 'Thanks.'

Jardin unhooked his coffee pot from over the flames and poured for his guest. He handed Carter a full cup.

Carter jerked his chin politely. 'Never thought I'd ever sit down like this with you, Ben, and like it.'

'That also goes twice,' Jardin replied. 'Have a fish. They're good trout. Nice and fat. They taste as good as salmon.'

'No, thanks,' Carter said, patting his stomach. 'Had me a chew on some salt beef as I came along.'

'You're welcome,' Jardin assured the other, smiling companionably. 'I've got some white bread and salt too.'

'You done at the Crippled Indian mine?'

Carter asked, declining a second time by gesture. 'I was told you had before I writ. Wouldn't have been so quick to suggest you come home otherwise.'

'Theakstone Mining has cleaned that rock out,' Jardin said.

'So you won't be going back to Cimarron Falls?'

'Done there, and drawn my time.'

'Good.'

Jardin looked at Carter a little narrowly. 'There's more, isn't there?'

'There is,' Carter acknowledged. 'I wanted to be sure you'd finished with Theakstone Mining before I broached it. Need you in the valley, d'you see?'

'Not really.'

'This is business, Ben.'

'Money business—or monkey business?'

'The first I'm sure of,' Carter said.

'But there could be a touch of the other?' Jardin inquired. 'Not sure I'm interested in that.'

'Oh, it's legal enough!' Carter protested. 'Others are doing it—with less cause than our families have. Yet I'm not sure it's

11

wholly right for all that.'

'What is it, Sam?'

'Tolling them Texans.'

'Tolling them—?' Jardin was briefly mystified, but the words spun around the inside of his head and quickly shaped their true sense. 'Making the Texas trailherders pay toll?'

'Like I said, tolling them Texans.'

'We have plenty of cattle drives coming up from Texas these days,' Jardin said judiciously, 'and they do mostly pass through Buffalo Valley—doing the hell-and-all damage to our crops.'

'You can say that again!' Carter snorted indignantly. 'You've had it over your side even worse than we've had it our'n. It's so bad this year, we're in two minds about next year's planting. Those longhorns from the Lone Star are breaking fences down and tearing all our crops up. If them drovers are going to ruin our harvests, I don't see why they shouldn't pay for it.'

'You have a point,' Jardin admitted, 'and it's a good one. To tell you the truth, Sam, my job with the mining company was taken last summer to pay for some of the losses those herds from Texas caused us last year. I was minded to put a flea in a trail boss's ear, but young Emma, my kid sister, the real wise head in our family, reminded me that those Texans are a wild lot and best left alone at any cost. You're a long time dead.'

'No denying that,' Carter conceded. 'Yet it's only when they hit town and get drink into them that those Southerners get dangerous to be around. Normally, they're hard men but fair. Meet 'em out on the prairie, when the herd's bedded down for the night and some fellow has got his squeeze-box out, and they're as reasonable as you or me.'

'Maybe,' Jardin said. 'I'd as soon whip the tail of a rattlesnake as go near a trail camp after dark!'

'Yes, you've got to mind what you're doing,' Carter admitted, 'but I've done it a few times and been treated real respectful. Them young Texans can be real nice boys, and you'll allow it's no picnic coming up from the Gulf.'

'Many of them do,' Jardin assented. 'So you think you can raise the wind from that direction?'

'They're making fortunes at the rail-heads, Ben,' Carter said. 'The buyers can't part with it fast enough. If it's hurting us, who've got so little, why shouldn't we have the crumbs of their plenty?'

'Because,' Jardin said grimly, 'human nature doesn't work like that. If a man's got money in his hand, he's sure he earned it to the last cent, and he doesn't like parting with any of it to somebody he's sure did nothing. As a rule, he'll fight.'

'Not a decent man who can see the harm he's done!' Carter protested. 'You're not like that—and I'm not like that! Mustn't be too hard when you sum folk up, Ben.'

'I'm not without my faults,' Jardin said. 'What were you thinking of?'

'Moneywise? Five cents a head?'

'Some of the herds coming through number three or four thousand head, Sam,' Jardin cautioned. 'You could be looking at two hundred dollars. That's a lot of money. Do it ten time a month, mister, and you're talking about two thousand dollars.'

'You're exaggerating, Ben!' Carter declared.

'Perhaps,' Jardin said. 'but only to make you stop and think. Why, two or three hundred dollars is as much as we'd expect our farms to make in a year. And a good one at that!'

'A herd running four thousand head,' Carter said stubbornly, 'can be worth a quarter of a million. A couple of hundred dollars is chickenfeed in that market. That being so, think of what's left to the rancher—even with all expenses paid. Other folk, in circumstances like to ours, are getting it, and why shouldn't we? It ain't a handout, Ben. If we go about it quietly, insistin' on our right, we'll get what we want.'

'You think so?'

''Pon my word we will!'

Jardin hunkered low. His doubts were shaken, though his fears stayed firm. The herds from Texas had indeed done great damage on the Jardin land, and the case for compensation had always been a strong one—though disregarded by the herders passing through on the grounds that they had a job to do and even more damage would result to property if they turned aside to argue cases. The claim that the central part of Buffalo Valley was common ground and therefore open to traverse by all was a legitimate one—and would unquestionably carry full weight in a court-of-law—but that could not excuse the damage inflicted on the farms along the route. When voracious longhorns broke herd and got among green crops, those crops were, to all practical intents and purposes, destroyed; and, with that at the middle of the argument and coupled to Sam Carter's contentious claims about Texan profits, it seemed reasonable to assert that the cattlemen from the South could easily afford to pay a handful of vulnerable Kansas farmers to let their land lie largely fallow in respect of the cattle drives each year. Yes, it all made sense, and Jardin found himself falling in with Sam Carter's point of view. No big admirer of Sam's intelligence before this, Jardin had to admit to himself that Carter had spotted the main chance way ahead of him and marshalled his facts into a case worthy of anybody's consideration. 'But they're going to say we're lazy,' Jardin finally let out under pressure from within, his head shaking slowly, 'and object to subsidising us in our idleness. It's a response a whole lot of other farmers will back, Sam. Man's a jealous critter, as you full well know, and he can't abide to see a fellow in the same job as himself come out better off without sweating for it. If the Texans threaten to shoot us up, you can bet your boots there'll be a host of our own kind who'll back 'em.'

'You're out then,' Carter said glumly.

'No, I'm in,' Jardin said reluctantly. 'But I'm not burning any bridges, Sam. Your case is a fair one, but it takes no account of human nature. We may be forced to back off. I've got my brothers Joe and Harry and their wives and little ones to think about; and you've got your sister Rosemary and brother Frank and his

17

wife and children to consider. First sign of real trouble, Sam, and we'll have to call it off—for everybody's sake. Right?'

'I suppose so,' Carter responded huffily. 'It ain't the kind of thinking I approve—it being weak. I said we didn't have to be warlike, didn't I? You can always get what you want if you're firm and in the right.'

'Yeah, that's the kind of high-falutin' talk you get from guys who've pulled it off,' Jardin agreed. 'Sadly, you don't hear much from the unsuccessful men. They're either long gone, too ashamed—crippled or dead.'

'So long as you're with me,' Carter said, standing up with a jerk. 'It's a start anyhow. If you'll be ruled by me—'

'I will, Sam,' Jardin promised—'for the start.'

Sighing, Carter offered his right hand this time. The movement was a trifle tentative, but Jardin was rising from the fireside to meet it, when a shot boomed from among the trees which bordered the nearby trail and the big man gave a shuddering start and grunted. Then he became stiff from top to toe and toppled across the fire like a felled tree, sparks, soot and smoke, gusting upwards around him in thick clouds from which Jardin retreated on staggering heels, his arms flung up to protect his face as he finally screwed away from the noisome eruption to his right.

Now Jardin was erect, gun in hand. He stood there rather stupidly, braced to receive more fire. But there was just the night vibrating about him, with its stars and crescent moon, and the nearby waters gurgling busily over the stones as they headed down country to join the greater flow of the Arkansas river a few dozen miles away.

Belatedly, and responding to a panicky surge of energy, Jardin went running towards the point from which he believed the fatal shot had come. His common sense told him that the bushwhacker had already slipped away, had a minute's start on him, and had probably got clear by now; but he ran onwards nevertheless and entered the trees, checking a little blindly as what light there had been before was cut off around him, and he came to the trail which traversed the heart of the timber and there stopped altogether, breath bated and ears listening intently.

A gasp burst from his chest as he discovered that he could interfere with his breathing no longer, and he started to pant, the blood hammering in his head and spoiling the attempted fine tuning of his eardrums. Though feeling baffled, he set off again, following some obscure instinct to which his senses had brought no clue, and slanted forward and to his right, arriving at the foot of a brush-clad slope that put another tuck in his thrusting haste.

Muscles bunched, he started ascending, the toes of his boots digging in, and his eyes turned back and he saw dim crags, a spectral presence, throwing up their silhouettes to the right of the moon's crescent and glowing just perceptibly here and there. Knee-deep in greasewood, Jardin bellied into a rock, and reeled aside, swearing under his breath. Then he stopped again, not from any hurt received but because a distinct noise had reached him from high above and instantly brought the picture to his mind of somebody climbing there. Yes, a slipping sole had unquestionably set some loose dirt and stones rolling, and now he could make out the sounds of recovery echoing down from the darkness that clothed the upper grade.

Jardin placed the climber's probable position with a nod. The man—since he naturally assumed that the killer was a man—could have lost his way after firing the fatal shot and now be seeking the trail. The other was almost certainly stepping sidewise to his right, and Jardin could think of no other reasonable explanation for such a curious action. It figured, then, that the bushwhacker had left a horse tethered at the trailside above the river before descending on the firelight of the campsite below. After that, with his bloody task achieved and a swift retreat essayed, it appeared that he had somehow missed the trail among the trees and ended up on the hillside beyond it. These things happened when haste and the night went together, and the unknown killer could have been trying to work out where he had gone wrong ever since.

Matching his own movements to what he imagined those of his unseen quarry to be, Jardin began side-stepping to his right and had not covered many yards when he felt the smooth, hard surface of the beaten way beneath his boots. Here the fringe of the trees once more created an umbrella of obscurity, but he pursued the rising path out of the timber's back until he reached the open about a hundred feet up the acclivity. Here, peering hard before him, he obtained an impression of the trail rising at an ever steeper angle towards a cleft in the ridge that he knew to separate the present neighbourhood from the Garden City area, and he supposed the bushwhacker to have reached this spot over the same route that he had himself followed here the previous evening.

Shifting his gaze, Jardin let his eye pass around the just perceptible curve of the low ridge from the southeast into the black smudge of the west. Gun in hand again, he resumed ascending, conscious that he could be climbing into danger, for the sounds of movement had ceased beneath the summit of the land adjacent, and wondered whether his own presence on the hillside had been detected when he had collided with the boulder during the earlier ascent that he had diverted eastwards.

It was possible that his quarry was crawling into position to meet him with a bullet. Yet that would be gifting the unknown man with cat's eyes, and a hunter could let himself get too cautious. Bearing that in mind, Jardin felt reasonably confident that, even if the other had sensed his presence in some way, the likelihood of an accurate shot being fired at him from ambush was not great. He and the other would have to stand virtually face to face before a telling shot could be fired.

Yet that, of course—as he abruptly realized—was precisely what he had had in mind for the last minute or two. He wanted to get within touching distance of Sam Carter's murderer and either blow a hole in him or flatten the hellion by any means of all. Jardin felt strange energies tremoring in his nape and solar plexus. A sensation of inadequacy grew in his mind with every step he trod. But this, he reminded himself, should not be. He had seen four years of service as a Union infantryman during the Civil War and done his fair share of creeping about in the brush and rocks at dead of night. The fact that he, a farmer for the most part, was out of practice in the skills of war, did not mean that he had never had them—or that his experience of tracking an enemy down in darkened country was less than the other man's. It might indeed be greater, for the unknown killer had already proved himself to be capable of mistakes and could well be so nervously strung up at present that he might even blunder into his enemy's hands before all was done.

Tense and utterly alert, Jardin tiptoed onwards and up. Then a horse snorted a short distance ahead and the spell was broken. Now Jardin heard hooves skitter and knew his man was mounting up. He lunged ahead, abandoning all caution as he assumed that the bushwhacker would be heading up the hill and away from him a moment or so from now, and was thus taken completely by surprise as he suddenly perceived the beast and its rider bearing down on him out of the dark.

Reacting as best he could, Jardin sprang away to his left; but, swiftly though he moved, the neck of the onrushing horse struck his right shoulder and sent him flying. He fell at the trailside, struck an unseen boulder, and flung back onto his left hip, revolver still firmly clutched in his hand. The escaping horseman was only a few yards away as yet, and Jardin made out a pale blur as a face came screwing round. Then two shots streaked redly at him, and he heard one bullet strike the trail beside him and felt the other tug at the right sleeve of his jacket.

Incensed, though badly winded, Jardin returned the fire, first forcing himself into a sitting position and then throwing his torso forward between his spread knees—thus placing himself in the best possible attitude for pumping shots after the fleeing rider—and he emptied his pistol at a speed that was not usual for him and heard the final detonation echoed by a cry of pain. He had made a hit all right—and felt the better for it—but had no means of telling how serious the wound could be, for the escaping horseman was already immersed in the pit of blackness at the bottom of the slope and to all practical intents and purposes clear and away.

Fumbling a reload as he sat there, Jardin breathed as slowly as he could and listened to the final rumour of the killer's departure; but, on clambering to his feet a minute later, felt a state of despondency come upon him such as he had not known in many a year. For a short while, down there by the stream, it had all come right—and that thrice-accursed blood feud had ended in handshakes and at least the possibility of mutual good—then it had all gone just as horribly wrong again. Sam Carter's murder in the present circumstances could prove the ultimate disaster for the Jardins and the Carters.

If ever in his life he had had the urge to run away, Ben Jardin had it now. But this had to be faced.

TWO

Jardin walked back down the hill to his campsite with a heavy tread. He found the spot by the water's-edge much as he had left it, though the last ashes of his fire were all but extinguished now and Sam Carter's body lay that trifle more relaxed. Hunkering down, Jardin struck another match and contemplated the huge corpse again, putting out a gentle hand and closing the dead man's eyes. He was mystified by what had taken place. What *had* happened here? Every man had his enemies—he had made a few himself across the years—but, even in these wild and lawless days, the kind of foes who wished to kill over the normal kind of disagreement were few and far between. So death had occurred here in regard of something far beyond the normal. And that made the whole thing even harder to guess at, for Sam Carter had been one of life's better men and less likely to get struck down from the night than Jardin himself.

Shutting out all but the event, Jardin brought his full mind to bear. No situation was without some clue; action itself indicated. He had assumed, in what he now realized had been a vague and woolly fashion, that the bushwhacker had ridden in from the Garden City district; but that could not have been, short of the circumstances being both remarkable and improbable, as Sam Carter must have ridden here on his mission of peace from somewhat south of east. On a reasonable assumption—since it was unlikely that a stay-at-home like Sam had often been this far away from Buffalo Valley—the actual motive for murder had been conceived close to home and the killer had pursued Sam to this spot in some kind of uncertainty as to whether the shooting should be carried out or not; so it was possible that either the actual meeting itself between Sam and himself—or something to do with it—had caused the fatal shot to be finally triggered. Anyway, the notion as a whole was unquestionably backed up by the direction in which the bushwhacker had made his getaway, for his charge downhill had contained a definite insistence on the compass point that he wished to reach—and further hinted at disturbed thinking—since, assuming that he had known Jardin was near him on the upper trail, his actual aims—whatever they were—would have been better served by riding northwards instead of south and later reversing course if necessary. Yes, it was safe to say that the direction of flight on which he had insisted provided what confirmation was required that he had shadowed Sam Carter here from Buffalo Valley.

Jardin took a new grip on his mind and went on with his close thinking. Factors that had been obscure at first now revealed themselves as obvious. It wasn't too much to say that somebody had known that Sam Carter was bent on burying the hatchet with the Jardins and didn't want the friendship between the families to be established. But who could that be?—and why? Buffalo Valley was the home of the Jardins and the Carters alone—and had been, indeed, since the second family had dogged the first from the feud-ridden mountains of Tennessee—and there was nobody at all in the vicinity who would care whether or not they killed each other. The only people living remotely nearby were the Harpers, and they occupied Blue Grass Valley, which was situated about four miles to the west of the valley in which the farmers lived and contained a business that had always appeared self-serving and uninterested in others to Jardin. For Dave Harper's Box H was a thriving ranch, and Harper had a contempt for tillers of the soil that kept him apart from the farmers of Buffalo Valley like nothing else could. True, there had been word out for years that the cattleman would be happy to buy up ground and expand; and he might well have the secret hope that the bloody-minded farmers would eventually destroy each other and leave their valley deserted for him to take over and use; but Jardin was prepared to swear that this had never been a serious issue with Dave Harper and that the man was not the sort of fool who would involve himself in any kind of subterfuge that threatened the Buffalo Valley farmers.

Straightening up again, Jardin grunted as he shook the stiffness out of knees that had been too long bent. There was much here to consider, but his thoughts were on the verge of becoming repetitive. Some of the material was strong, yet too much of it was weak. He was tired, and doubted that he could get much out of his analysis right now. Not that he had any prospect of rest. Corpses didn't keep, and he had one to get home before it started to decompose. If he rode the clock round twice, he ought to reach Buffalo Valley and the Carter farm by tomorrow evening. It was going to be a rough go, but he had had enough of being driven to the limit in his life to accept it as

31

a frequent necessity. At the end of it, he would either die of a Carter bullet or sleep long and deeply in his own bed at home. But a grim scene at the Carter place would be impossible to avoid, and the chance that Frank and Rosemary Carter would believe that somebody other than he had slain their elder brother was not strong. At best, the grief that he must bear to them was such that he could himself hardly stand it just then. They were to be pitied.

He squared his shoulders. It had to be done; the duty was his alone, and he really must get on with it. If he did what was right, heaven might protect him—though he had little faith in help from that direction—and again he stepped out towards the trees, trying to guess at what point Sam Carter had left his horse before pausing at the edge of the campsite and watching the man in the firelight beside the stream.

Re-entering the trailside timber, Jardin located Carter's mount within a minute. He gave the brute a pat on the neck and spoke a friendly word in its ear. Already restive, the horse chucked away from him at first, but soon settled to his hand and allowed him to lead it towards the spot where its dead master lay. Halting the creature beside the corpse, Jardin untied the bedroll from behind Carter's saddle and found that the blankets were wrapped in a waterproof coat. Opening out the slicker—then using the blankets as an inner covering—he shrouded the dead man with the utmost care and buttoned the waterproof about him, exerting his own great strength after that and lifting the body into an upright position from which he was able to pitch it forward and over the saddle that had borne it in life. Then, as the final security, he tied it down with Carter's lariat and made a neat job of it all by tucking in the loose ends of oilskin and rope.

Next, leaving the burdened horse, he recovered his frying pan and coffee pot, throwing away what was left of their spoiled contents. Then he washed them out at the water's-edge and carried them to where his own mount stood among the nearby jackpines, stowing them in an open saddlebag and buckling down. Now he mounted up and, riding over to Carter's horse, caught up its reins in his left hand and put pressure on the leathers as he prodded his own mount into faster motion. With the second horse coming along smoothly, he regained the trail; then, making a left turn, he approached the ford in the nearby flow and crossed over, following the beaten way southwards after that and working up to a steady trot. 'Sorry, mister,' he said to his black gelding, 'this is going to be tough. But there's no other way?'

Only taking such rests as were vital, they travelled through the night and into the morning. Fatigue hit Jardin with full force around the breakfast hour, and for a time he was all but asleep in the saddle, but he perked up again as the sun climbed—finding that his horse seemed to do the same—and they journeyed on by fits and starts into the spring day, the purplish-green of the Kansas plain spreading wide on every hand and the sky falling hugely from its middle blue into buttermilk edges that were always there and appeared to take no account of the aching miles.

The horses were almost begging for mercy, and Jardin's turnip said the time was a quarter to five in the afternoon, when he spotted the town of Standish away to his left and knew that he was nearing home. Standish occupied a piece of ground between the Blue Grass and Buffalo valleys, and represented Saturday night and the source of supplies for all the folk within a radius of fifty miles. The town also had a sheriff—Abe Holst, an officious little cuss with a long nose and a far-seeing eye—so Jardin decided to give the place a wide berth, for he had no desire to explain the dead body on his second horse and figured it only right that he should leave it to the Carter family to decide whether or not they should call in the law after they had the remains of Big Sam in their keeping. Explanations could be made to Abe Holst then, if they had to be.

With the haze of tiredness again enveloping him, and his horse often stumbling—

while the one to his rear drooped and sweated—Jardin finally completed his ride home. He dropped down into Buffalo Valley with the full prospect of the place flowing before him under the oblique rays of the evening light. He saw first the Carter farm crouching on his fairly immediate right, and then his own home—about a mile further on—nestling closer to the valley wall on his left. He would normally have felt delight at the scene, with its sprawling miles of rough grass and uneven, mottled confines; but now, between his utter fatigue and the depression he felt at what lay before him, he could have easily drawn his pistol, put it to his head, and blown out his brains. Yet beyond this could be said that, as his imminent arrival at the Carter farm got fully through to him, fear of what might soon happen brought on a rush of blood that restored his energies and drove away the clouds from his mind. In fact he felt almost normal as he contemplated what he was going to say. After all, he had no reason to be afraid, for he had shaken Sam's hand in friendship and done the best that he could in hopelessly adverse circumstances thereafter.

Slanting eastwards for the farmhouse, Jardin steered out of the great swathe of cow tracks which had been cut down the valley's centre by the herds from Texas and closed on the ploughed land beyond. Back straight, he let his tired eyes seek, and suddenly glimpsed movement at a downstairs window of the house. Within seconds, the front door of the dwelling opened and a young woman appeared on the step. She was taller than average, and had hair that was truly as black as the raven's wing. Her features were large, yet delicately imprinted on the pale oval of her face, and the hand that she raised sharply to her mouth was long-fingered and beautifully shaped. Despite their being English farming stock, Jardin had heard the tale that aristocratic blood had got into the Carter lineage—no doubt way back and through some reckless son of the gentry—and just then, disregarding all else that he had on his mind,

Jardin could have believed the tale, for Rosemary Carter could in that moment easily have been some great lady come to look out upon the world. 'Ben?' she called doubtfully. 'What—what have you got there? That—that's Sam's horse!'

Jardin made no reply but, using the untilled strip between two fields planted with maize, he continued closing on her—and she came out of the house and slowly closed on him, both hands at her mouth now and an expression of horror growing on those features that were as perfect as her big brother's had been the reverse. 'What has happened, Ben?' she asked brokenly, when they halted about two yards apart. 'Is he—?'

'You can see,' Jardin returned blankly.

'Did you two get quarrelling again?'

'No, we did not, Rosemary,' Jardin said shortly. 'We'd shaken hands, and were getting on tophole—because Sam and I never did dislike each other that much—when somebody up and shot him out of the night. He died instantly, and it was horrible. I ran after the varmint who did it, and eventually put a bullet in him; but I couldn't have hurt the hellion that much—because he got away on horseback. There's detail, sure, but that's all of it which matters.'

'I knew Sam had gone to meet you,' Rosemary Carter said. 'He told me about it—though not Frank and Adah.'

Jardin nodded his understanding, then dismounted at the girl's signal. 'He told you why he wanted to speak with me alone? About what he had in mind for the Jardins and his own family, I mean?'

'Not before he left,' the girl replied. 'But he had spoken of it to me before, and I I guessed A wink is as good as a nod to—'

'I know,' Jardin assured her, as she paused.

'Where did it happen?'

'Beside a stream—about a dozen miles this side of Garden City.'

'When exactly?'

'Early last night.'

'So you've come about eighty miles since then.'

'Give or take. I—I pushed it, Rosemary. You can guess why.'

'Brother Frank will go crazy!'

'That's what I'm afraid of,' Jardin admitted. 'Do what you can, control him, I beg of you. We don't want any more blood spilled over this. We've damned nearly wiped out each other's family now. Before God, it happened exactly as I told you! We even had a sort of agreement to try slapping a toll on the Texans.'

'He probably told you how I felt about that one?'

'I reckon I feel about the same—and for similar reasons, I'd guess—but the cause is just.'

'Yes, the cause is just,' Rosemary Carter acknowledged drearily. 'But death ends all causes.'

'Aye, that's the catch,' Jardin agreed.

'Will you—will you bring him indoors, Ben?'

'I'll do that for you,' Jardin said, going to the exhausted horse which bore the heavy corpse and starting to pull at the knots. 'Where'll you want him?'

'Through in the kitchen,' Rosemary answered. 'He's got to be laid out somewhere. The table will do. You'll have only to follow me.'

'Right,' Jardin said, the main knots quickly falling to his fingers and the lesser ones doing the same. 'Poor guy.'

'Yes.'

With the rope which had secured the body lying on the ground beneath the belly of the dead man's horse, Jardin took Sam Carter's remains upon his shoulders, still shrouded by the blankets and slicker, and carried them towards Rosemary. Turning away from him, she soon regained the front of the house and entered at the still open door, and Jardin followed her in and passed down the length of the hall at her heels, coming to the rooms at the back of the building. Here they entered the kitchen, and the girl hastily cleared away the cooking utensils which lay upon the scrubbed top of the table at its centre.

That much done, Jardin laid the body upon the table-top as gently as he could. Then he unshrouded it. Now Sam Carter lay there in a state of rigor mortis, a bloodstained and far from pleasant sight that also smelled of a faint corruption produced by the day's heat within the closely binding blankets and waterproof coat. Trying to keep every trace of disgust off his features, Jardin stepped back, also heavily suppressing a desire to spit. 'I'll help you with this, Rosemary,' he said.

'There's my sister-in-law, Adah,' the dark girl reminded. 'She's out the back, playing with her children.'

'I knew Adah Wilkins,' Jardin said bluntly. 'She's no good for a job like this. It needs a hard couple like you and me to clear up this kind of mess.'

At that very instant the back door opened and a soft-eyed, brown-haired woman entered—her gaze instantly widening as it came to rest upon the table and her hands flying above her head as she screamed at the top of her voice.

'Adah!' Rosemary remonstrated. 'Pull yourself together!'

'But he's—!' the other woman choked, reeling back outside and beginning to sob hysterically with the door pulled to between her and what she obviously couldn't face.

'You stop that and come in here!' Rosemary ordered. 'It's happened, Adie, and we can't alter it!'

'She can't help it,' Jardin said. 'Tell her to go back to her kids.'

Then the back door flung inwards again and a big, lank, tow-headed man came spluttering into the kitchen, an axe in his hands and a wild, frightened look in his pale blue eyes. He, too, stared at the table, an indescribable expression of horror building upon his knobbly, sharp-nosed features, and then he gazed at Jardin—a sort of comprehension appearing to flood his shocked mind—and the light upon his face became that of one half mad. Next moment he flung up his axe and flew at Jardin, jaws spilling fluid as he yelled: 'I'll do for you, you murderin' son-of-a-bitch!'

Jardin backed off. The moment was a fraught one, yet it was really his, for all he had to do was draw his revolver and threaten or even shoot his attacker.

43

Instead, he halted at the threshold of the hall and raised staying palms. 'Hold it, Frank!' he pleaded. 'You've got this all wrong!'

Rosemary Carter also called on her brother to desist, then tried to intervene, but was elbowed heavily aside. Frank had obviously lost all control of himself, and he kept up his charge. His axe on the whirl, he rounded the table and struck at Jardin with all his force, but his intended victim swayed away from the blow and the blade of the tool made contact with the connecting door on Jardin's right and reduced its top half to splinters.

Perceiving that his would-be killer was momentarily off balance, Jardin knew that he must act fast. Springing forward, he punched over the angled haft of the axe, burying his right fist up to the wrist in Frank Carter's solar plexus; then, as the other doubled forward with eyes popping, let go the hardest left hook that he could manage to wind-up in his tired state. The blow landed squarely on the side of the big farmer's jaw, and Frank Carter fell as if he had indeed been shot. He lay sprawled upon his back, all the colour drained from his cheeks and clearly out for the count. 'I'm sorry, Rosemary!' Jardin declared, picking up the anger and loathing in her face as he cast a glance towards her. 'What would you have had me do? Was I to shoot him? I did the only thing I could!'

'Get out of here, Ben!' Rosemary ordered. 'Get out of here, please—before Frank comes round!'

'All right,' he said, screwing round on his heel and then calling across his shoulder: 'Remember, I'm no enemy of yours; and a friend if you need one.'

'Just go!'

That was definite enough, and Jardin walked out of the house smarting a little. Going straight to his horse, he swung back into the saddle and drew his brute's head round to the left, missing the late Sam Carter's drooping mount by a yard or more as he middled the strip of uncultivated ground between the two fields of maize and spurred for the trampled earth of the common ground where the herds from

Texas appeared to have been passing with some regularity again this year.

His horse, smelling home as surely as its master did, put in an effort of its own and Jardin let it run, doing little more than hold the reins. His angled ride had taken him well past the valley's middle, when a shot cracked out in his wake. He looked back, careful not to check his horse, and a second detonation roared as his eyes came to rest on the spot—at the limit of the Carter property and opposite their front door—where the long-bodied Frank, duly recovered from his sock on the jaw, was aiming what looked like an old Henry rifle at the recent visitor to his house and doing his best to fire an accurate shot.

While by no means happy at being a target, Jardin smiled sourly to himself. That ancient Army gun had just about the range to reach him at this stage of his ride, but he hadn't a doubt that the unquestionably groggy Frank stood around one chance in a hundred thousand of hitting him. So, still looking back, he rode on as before, listening as the rifle banged a third and fourth times without putting a slug anywhere near him. His only regret was that Frank Carter's behaviour was clearly setting the pattern for a hostile future. But, before the farmer could trigger a fifth shot, his sister Rosemary appeared at his elbow and snatched the rifle from him, a right index finger wagging as she upbraided her murderous sibling in what looked like no uncertain terms.

Well, there was hope in that; how much, he couldn't say; nor did he want to think about it any more today. He wished only to close his eyes and go to sleep. If virtue must be its own reward, his recompense had surely been slight enough of late.

THREE

There was in Ben Jardin this morning, as he sat at the breakfast table—with the house buzzing around him as the women did their cleaning—a feeling that he no longer had a place here. He had been away for too many months, of course, and the folk he'd left behind him had formed their own patterns of living, domestic and otherwise, as he knew very well folk always would. This home didn't need him as its head any longer; it had brothers Joe and Harry to direct things, and the women could think for themselves too; especially young Emma, his kid sister, who reminded him more and more of their dead mother every time she opened her mouth to speak.

It wasn't that the family weren't deferring to him, or that they didn't appreciate the hard-earned dollars that he had brought home—even that he wasn't being waited on like the monarch of all he surveyed—for the underlying trouble was more subtle than any of that. It had to do with collective character—of a unit formed to face and exploit the world—with the tightened family sheer and absolute, and he just didn't seem to fit or have what it took any more. Nor, perhaps, even want to; and that was an even worse feeling, when you got right down to it. True, he had been away for spells before—and experienced something of this same faint sense of rejection and uneasiness when he had got home again—but, give it an hour or two previously, and it had faded away and he had taken his place as head of the household once more as if he had never been away.

Finishing the last of his eggs, bacon, and fried bread, Jardin pushed his plate aside and drew to him the stone mug that contained his honey-sweetened coffee. He drank deeply, but with less than his usual relish—and it was then that he had to admit to himself that he had a hangover. Not the alcoholic kind, since he hadn't touched strong drink in weeks, but the sort that came from too much wakefulness and activity followed by too much inertia and sleep. After getting indoors yesterday evening, he had eaten and drunk almost nothing, spoken briefly and to the point of his meeting with Sam Carter and the subsequent tragedy: warned that new trouble could visit them from across the valley, and then gone to bed and fallen asleep almost instantly, remaining thus unconscious for the next thirteen hours. A guy really couldn't snore his head off from seven o'clock in the evening until eight the next morning without suffering for it. But did that answer for what he felt to be wrong here? It did not. He remained in some sense the odd man out, and felt a strong urge to get back into the open, where he could again possess his own soul and be answerable to nobody. Least of all himself!

For he could not divorce himself from his own home and family on the whim. He was preoccupied with his feelings, but nobody had said a word that disquietened. His responsibility was still there—and he could indeed be wrong about everything else. Like as not, the rest would be amazed if they knew what was going on inside his head. They might well prescribe a ride to blow the cobwebs out, and that was what he needed. Brother Joe had said last evening that Tom Tupper, the well-known trail-boss, was heading this way with a large herd of whitefaces from the Trinity river country in Texas. He'd ride out and meet with Tupper—have a serious talk with the guy, who carried much weight among his fellows—and see whether he couldn't arrange to extract some kind of payment from the drovers against the present and future harm which the Texas herds would inevitably cause in Buffalo Valley. If Sam Carter had had the guts to try for justice, he saw no reason why he should not show a little backbone too. He was a reasonable man, none more so, and he also had a greater gift than most for understanding and co-operation. If Tom Tupper could produce an argument which clearly showed that the herders should not be held responsible for the damage their charges did to the farms along their path, he would back off and shut up. But he'd be damned if he could see right now what that argument was to be. Indeed, the longer he thought about it, the more sure he became that Sam Carter had been right. Some compensation was due, and the best way of exacting that would be through a toll on the herds. Was it a way of making easy money? Well, yes. But it was also true that the Texas ranchers were making a lot of easy money too. Why, the income off one big herd could keep a cattleman in comfort for the rest of his days. All things were relative but, in these times, a hundred thousand dollars was the clover patch. Nor was a hundred thousand dollars anywhere in it with what the Slaughters and the Chisums were raking in. They'd die millionaires many times over!

His coffee mug emptied, Jardin pressed himself erect from the table. It was then that he realized his sister Emma, the baby of the family, had been hovering close to the living room door throughout his meal. 'Any more, Ben?' she asked, coming in to him, her pink cheeks seeming to exactly match the thick yellow of her hair—so much like his own—and the deep blue of her merry eye.

'No thanks,' he said, grinning. 'I'm stuffed to the gills. We didn't get fed by Theakstone Mining the way you women feed us.'

'A working man needs good meals,' his sister averred.

'No doubt about that,' Jardin allowed— 'though I'm not sure I rate as a working man just now. Emma, I'm going to take a leisurely ride down the country today.'

'You do that, Ben,' the girl approved. 'But your horse is no shape for it.' She considered him with a fond eye. 'You can use mine. Old Buck could do with some exercise.'

'Thanks,' he said. 'I will. That poor varmint of mine took a beating yesterday. Enough to kill him, if I do say so myself, after the soft life he'd been having in the barn. But there you are. It had to be, sis. I had to get Sam Carter home while he was still fresh enough to handle.'

'It's a good job Frank and Adah have children,' Emma said. 'The Carter family would be ended if it wasn't for that.'

'Yes,' Jardin agreed. 'It's just a pity that the fathering's been done by the least member of the Carter family.'

'Sam would never have married,' Emma said.

'Why not?'

'He was too ugly—and too big.'

'They do say women aren't that fussy,' Jardin growled. 'I don't think that can be right. Trouble is, I suppose, we've still so few females in this neck-o'-the-woods, they can pick and choose.'

'No problem for you,' the girl observed archly. 'You're right handsome.'

'You could be prejudiced, Emma.'

'No, brother.'

'Well, if I stand favourably in female sight, it's never noticed.'

'You go around with your eyes shut, Ben,' Emma chided. 'The very girl for you lives right across the valley. Heaven made her.'

'Rosemary Carter!' Jardin scoffed, embarrassed despite himself. 'She sent me packing yesterday evening, and she boxed my ears once in town.'

'They say the Good Lord chastiseth those he loveth best,' Emma laughed. 'Women are like that too.'

'The feud's still on, Emma.'

'Nonsense!' the girl retorted. 'It was

over the day old man Carter died. Sam was always a friend; mother liked him. As for Frank and Adah—Rosemary says what goes there. So stop looking downcast.'

'Do you want to get rid of me, Emma?'

'Only to where your happiness lies, Ben,' Emma answered gravely. 'And maybe happiness for the rest of us too. What chance would there ever be of that feud flaring up again with you and Rosemary together?'

'It had occurred to me,' Jardin admitted. 'But let's not romance, eh? It takes two hearts to make a bargain. I don't guess Rosemary is much in love with me today.' He laughed aloud, brightening distinctly inside. 'How about you and a band of gold, sis? You're nineteen. That's almost an old maid in Buffalo Valley!'

'I'll get there,' the yellow-haired girl promised, her voice full of an unshakeable confidence. 'Now if you have finished in here, I'd like to clear away and do the washing up.'

Jardin nodded and, going over to the door which gave access to the stairs, took down his gunbelt from one of the wooden pegs which jutted there. Swinging the belt around his waist, he buckled it into place and eased his Colt in the holster.

'Be careful,' Emma urged from behind him, rattling the cutlery and the plates.

'How's that again?' Jardin asked quickly.

'You're going to meet Tom Tupper and his herd, aren't you?'

Jardin hesitated. 'As a matter of fact, I am.'

'It was plain to me, Ben. What else would you want to ride afield for after all the way you've come?'

'I shouldn't try to keep anything from you, should I?'

'Nor Rosemary.'

'I suppose you girls have got each other weighed to the ounce.'

'Are you men so different?'

'Well, we're supposed to be smarter. Our heads measure more around them.'

'Isn't that the truth!' Emma declared, catcalling. 'If little girls didn't take care of little boys from the word go, there wouldn't be any of them grow up!'

'Then there wouldn't be any little girls either,' Jardin reminded sagely. 'None of us have that long, sis—and nineteen really is pushing that old canoe out. Heavens, girl—you'll be twenty before you know it and cutting yourself a stick!'

Carrying a pile of plates and cutlery before her, Emma walked through to the kitchen, laughing and, acknowledging her disdainful merriment with a sardonic grin of his own, Jardin moved to the front door and let himself out of the house. He glanced around him, mainly inspecting the sky, as he closed up in his wake, then, having decided that it was going to be a nice day, walked round the house to the stables and entered there by opening the lower section of the halved door.

Noting at once that his own horse had been fed and curried by a member of the family, he went to the stall where his sister Emma's gelding stood and dressed the animal with the saddle and reins that lay upon the tack rail adjacent. After that he led the brute outside and into the grass of the valley floor, where he swung up and kept a check on the bit as he looked southwards. The slight climb towards the plain beyond invited and he launched out, encouraging the briefly thwarted Buck to canter, and soon he was up land of the farm buildings and opposite the Carter place at the other side of the valley.

He noted movement over there from the tail of his eye, but didn't turn his head—since he had no intention of doing the smallest thing to encourage trouble—and simply rode on, topping the land crest ahead within a minute or two and then gazing on into the pale distance under the big sky, conscious of fading horizons and the small eternity of miles that came at last to warm seas and a different space, where ships plied the blowing oceans and his valley had no dreams to match those of lands which had been old in legend before his own first felt history's touch. He had travelled after by the standards of his day, yet knew that he led a restricted life, and he had to clamp down on his yearning for journeys to see places and things that his inner man told him he had not been meant to see in this lifetime. There was a certain frustration in it and, with this added to his doubts and problems, he felt his mood darkening again and his earlier confidence that he could match Tom Tupper in peaceful argument on the wane. These Texans were hard men, and what they had they held. That had been his original thinking, and so ran his mind again. He was courting trouble, and it would be wiser to go back home; but he rode on through the fragrance of the grass and the light of the morning.

Thus, lost in his own thoughts, Jardin gave a slight start when, presently, he heard a horse galloping up behind his own; and he turned his head and peered back with a narrowed eye, his right hand ready for trouble if it had to be; but he saw Rosemary Carter approaching on a shaggy old swayback which her family often used for ploughing and slowed to let her catch up with him. 'Morning,' he greeted, determined to keep it affable if he could. 'It looks like we've got ourselves a nice day, hey?'

'Yes,' the dark girl agreed, a neat figure in her red shirt and black riding skirt. 'Good morning, Ben. You still look three-parts worn out.'

'Oh, the horses got the worst of it,' he disclaimed. 'How's Frank?'

'None the worse. Hurt in the pride, if anywhere.'

'I've been hurt there myself,' Jardin admitted. 'I don't always win.'

'Do you have to fight at all?'

He hesitated, passing from the glib reply to a moment's hard thought. 'It can't always be avoided, Rosemary. This isn't a perfect world. Some men just feel they were born to have and ride roughshod.'

'I saw you ride past, Ben, and have half a notion of where you're bound.'

'That sister Emma of mine had a whole one.'

'Emma's a little special.'

'She feels the same about you,' Jardin said, putting his tongue firmly in his cheek. 'I have a suspicion she wants you for a sister-in-law.'

'She what!'

'I told her you might have other thoughts about that one.'

'We buried Sam in the family plot behind the sheds yesterday evening,' Rosemary said soberly. 'He's lying at mother's left hand, and the children are carrying flowers to his grave and crying over him.'

'Sure, you can do without poor jokes this morning,' Jardin said contritely. 'It seems you want to tag along. That was the idea?'

'Tom Tupper is coming up the trail, isn't he?'

'That's what they say. The word sure carries. From what I was told last evening, we ought to run across his herd before noon.'

'He should be closer than that,' Rosemary said. 'From what I was told yesterday, much closer.'

'We'll see.'

'Yes, I have to take Sam's place now.'

'There's no "have to" about it,' Jardin reminded. 'There's Frank.'

'He's better with his hoe.'

'We could be headed for trouble.'

'That's something I'd like to keep both of us out of, Ben.'

'It isn't a wise venture,' Jardin sighed. 'Yet I can't make it a wrong one.'

'It isn't wrong, but it is indeed unwise —and we had need be circumspect.'

'Big word, Rosemary.'

'I'll bet you know what it means.'

'I do.'

'You'll let me do my share of the talking?'

'More,' Jardin assured her—'if it so shapes.' Then he decided to be entirely open about his feelings of that moment. 'Guess I'm a bit of a toad for saying this, but a woman always has a better chance in a money argument with a man than another man has. Guys don't like to be thought tight-fisted by gals.'

'That's rather calculating, Ben.'

'Didn't I say, it makes me a toad?'

'It may also,' the girl said, smiling to herself, 'be true.'

'Yeah,' he drawled, knowing that they understood each other well enough.

That appeared to set a seal on their

talk for the moment. They rode on in thoughtful silence, and perhaps another quarter of an hour had gone by, when Jardin glimpsed a thin but extensive dustcloud rising above the countryside a mile or two away on his right and quickly pointed it out to his companion. 'That's a big herd over yonder, Rosemary,' he said. 'It's got to be Tom Tupper's. There's no news of a second one in the neighbourhood right now.'

'Can they have missed their way?' the dark girl wondered, frowning as she gazed down at the wide, hoof-torn scar upon the plain ahead of them. 'I wouldn't have thought that possible.'

'It isn't,' Jardin returned. 'That's Tupper to the west of us, you may be sure, and he's deliberately missing Buffalo Valley for some reason.'

'He's going to take his herd through Blue Grass.'

It was on the tip of Jardin's tongue to say that he did not believe it. But seeing was still believing. And, with a curious feeling under his heart that mingled relief and a certain mortified annoyance, he reined in and settled forward in his seat, brow gathering as he sought an explanation of what was happening. 'This makes no sense!' he finally declared. 'Blue Grass Valley is the home of the Box H ranch. Dave Harper has got cows all over the auction. Yes, the Blue Grass is a much wider valley than ours—and it could be cleared back to make a broad corridor along its eastern side; but can you imagine Harper doing it?'

'I remember it once being done during the Civil War, Ben,' the girl said, 'while you were away. As for imagining it now, I've got to. The Blue Grass Valley is the only alternative cow route through this part of Kansas to our own valley. What between the blocking hills and rivers in this district, the herds would have to divert by miles and miles to get to the railheads if they missed us entirely.' She clucked in irritation. 'Oh, what *are* we to make of it? Unless—'

Jardin glanced round at her quickly. 'Unless what?'

'It has something to do with Sam's murder.'

'Like what then?'

'He was shot for some reason, Ben,' Rosemary said. 'Unless the killer was really out to get you. I don't know all the details, do I? You must agree there are things here I've been taking on trust.'

'I agree with that,' he returned. 'There are details you don't know, and you've got your share of imagination. If the bushwhacker had really been out to get me, Rosemary, he could hardly have missed me at the first. Both Sam and I were in the light of my campfire—both clear shots.' He gave his head a brief, hard little shake. 'No. If the killer had had any designs on me at all, he could have got me with a second shot. He had ample time for that. It was Sam he was after okay—and, yes, there has to be a reason for the murder.'

'What about to stir up the feud again?' Rosemary Carter hazarded. 'Could you see Texas cowmen driving herds through a valley where local farmers were shooting at each other? Or even where there was a danger of that happening?'

'No,' Jardin said uncertainly. 'Your thinking's clever all right, Rosemary, and Dave Harper could be scheming to bring the Texas herds through his valley on payment of toll. But that would be dog-eat-dog. Harper's name would stink clear across the South. I don't see it. He'd have more to lose than gain; and there wouldn't be enough money in it for the likes of him anyhow.'

'It's got to be the answer, Ben!' Rosemary declared. 'Nothing else makes any sense at all! I've got a good mind to visit Abe Holst, the sheriff in Standish, and tell him what happened to Sam and what I now think about it! Sam's murder ought to be avenged!'

'So it did,' Jardin said, keeping cool in face of her fierceness. 'Going to the sheriff is up to you. I was determined to leave it so. But do remember, please, that Sam was gunned down far outside our man's jurisdiction. His case is really a Federal case. And who're you actually going to accuse? I've not a doubt that Sam's murder was cooked up in this district; but, on what little evidence we have of that at present, it would be difficult to prove this day from Sunday week. It could even turn out to be a coincidence. Now and again the Tuppers and the Harpers of this life get together to make things easier for themselves.'

'You're telling me to do nothing!' Rosemary accused.

'You're free to do what the devil you please!' Jardin retorted. 'It's simply that I don't see what you're going to do at present. We have nothing but suspicions to serve up. They're a hell of a lot of good! You go to the law with a story that you can't start to prove, and the law will go off you in a mighty big way. Maybe I'm saying don't cry wolf—yet.'

'Isn't it possible that we know all now we're going to know?'

'Give it time,' Jardin urged; but he couldn't deny it outright, and he drew himself upright in the saddle, looking glum. 'I don't know what else to tell you, Rosemary.'

She pulled a face at this eventual

addition, then fired in a trifle sarcastically. 'That's best for you—or me?'

'Is it that you're not absolutely sure that I wasn't responsible for Sam's death?' he asked, stung. 'Or is it that you blame me for not being able to see round corners or hear voices at a hundred miles? Truth will out.'

'It usually does,' she agreed—'when it's too late to matter. Well, it's no good riding after Tom Tupper now. That scheme is quashed for today. I'm turning for home. Are you coming?'

'No,' he responded. 'I've done little but swing a pick and push a shovel since the end of last summer. I feel the need for a little freedom. I guess I'll go into town, and maybe have a beer. Perhaps I'll catch word of what's happening yonder in the process.'

'That sounds like your father,' Rosemary scoffed. 'What self-indulgent creatures you men are! No work to be done back home? What kind of husband would you make?'

'Be thankful you'll never have to find out,' Jardin advised her, yanking his horse away to the right and then setting off across the land closer to north than west. He had had a gutful of it so far this morning, and Rosemary had added insult to injury. It could be that he ought to find some quiet corner miles from anywhere and just sit down and watch the grass grow. This day did not augur well at all.

FOUR

It seemed to Jardin, as he rode slowly down the main street, that the town of Standish had not changed by a single detail since he had last visited it a big piece of a year ago. Every stain, broken strut, rusty hinge and cobweb was as before, and the dust upon the windows contained the same largely formless traceries as he recalled from the August gone. Even the horse droppings and the garbage lying about had the same appearance, given that the frosts of winter had broken the one up some and

69

put a coating of rust on much of the other. Standish was a frankly insalubrious rathole, but it was alive in all respects, money was changing hands, music jangled—even at this hour—booze was gurgling down a variety of throats, and there could be no doubt that sweaty love was being made in the bedrooms of the bawdy houses. This was the West, for the spirit of the frontier had long ago moved on. The apathy of the years had settled here, as elsewhere, and the dust and tedium were as much part of the torpid will to survive as anything else. When Abraham Standish—whoever the deuce he might have been—had given his name to this Kansas town, he had dignified a rubbish dump. Or not, maybe, depending on how you saw it, since Man had always been prone to ignore his own shortcomings.

Jardin reined in and dismounted outside the Hellgate saloon. There were other watering places in town, yes, but this was the biggest and the best—always relatively speaking—and here congregated the local gossips, know-alls, and bigwigs:

not to mention troublemakers, cardsharps, bunco-dealers, drummers and the like; altogether, a fair cross-section of their time and place. Sometimes exciting, the Hellgate was never dull, could be dangerous, and was invariably costly; but Jardin had never yet met with trouble in there and reckoned that enjoying a beer within its walls depended on no more than behaving yourself. Let other folk say their say and make a noise; he was always prepared to sit and listen, and would be even more so this morning.

Entering the saloon through the bat-wings, Jardin found himself immersed in a faintly sour atmosphere that was still thick with last night's tobacco smoke; and the flat tones of the faro dealer and the slow but sharp clicking of the chuck-a-luck wheel came at once to his ears. Walking up to the bar, he stood silent and waited for the yawning, big-bellied Gordon Sturgess—who was polishing a glass and staring at nothing in particular—to become aware of his waiting presence. The barman took a full minute to spot him, then shambled up, after putting down the glass and polishing cloth, as if tomorrow would do. 'Ben,' he acknowledged. 'Long time no see.'

'Been up Smoky Hill way,' Jardin explained. 'Had a job with Theakstone Mining.'

'Heard about it. Finished now?'

'Yes.'

'Well, there's the farm.'

'There's always that.'

'What's it to be?'

'A mug of light beer.'

Nodding, Sturgess took down a glass mug from a shelf on the backbar and held its lip to the spigot of a barrel chocked up on the end of the divide just a pace or so to the right. The suds streamed out fresh and misty yellow, and Jardin put a quarter down in payment and then lifted his drink, quaffing with open pleasure, since he was thirsty and the beer satisfied his palate. 'Good?' Sturgess asked, smiling.

'Damned good!' Jardin acknowledged. 'We were allowed none at the Crippled Indian mine, and didn't get out much.'

'Not much of a life like that, Ben, but these rules have got to be, I suppose.'

'A drunk's a menace to himself and everybody else,' Jardin reflected. 'Especially in a mine. The accidents I've seen through strong drink! But—I reckon it's all right in its place.'

'It's my living,' the barkeeper said, shrugging the shrug of a man who wondered what else he would be expected to say. 'I've got last Saturday's *Denver Chronicle*. Want it? I know you've always been a reading man, and guys like you don't change their habits.'

'I like to keep up with the news,' Jardin replied—'for what good it does. Can't change much, can we?'

Sturgess grinned mechanically, his puffy cheeks tinged an unhealthy purple and black, protuberant eyes dull beneath their shaggy brows. Then he started to look around—obviously for the newspaper mentioned—and finally called out: 'Who's got my Denver newspaper? There's a guy here who wants a read of it!'

A man's wide back moved at a big

round table over in the further right-hand corner of the bar-room; and, idly conscious that there were eight or ten other men sitting in company with the one who'd stirred, Jardin took little real notice when the original figure screwed round and tossed a loosely rolled newspaper onto the top of an unoccupied table which was situated equidistant between his own and the divide at which Jardin stood. Then, to Jardin's surprise, a voice that was distinctly familiar, if not heard for many a day, shouted to the barkeeper in a jeering manner: 'He can't read, mister! He wouldn't know a woodcut from a charleyhorse!'

A faintly knowing smile upon his features, Jardin turned now towards the speaker and, as expected, saw craning at him the swarthy, narrow-chinned face of George Roscoe, a wartime comrade of his in the Second Ohio Regiment of Volunteers —and a man whose guts he had frankly hated, for the other was a thief and a bully, and those were the best of his attributes.

'Hello, George,' he said. 'What are you

doing in these parts?'

'Minding my own business, Ben,' Roscoe responded.

'You can't do better than that,' Jardin approved.

'You?'

'The very same,' Jardin answered, hoping Roscoe had so much on hand about him that this talk would peter out on the general and inconsequential before getting too specific or intimate.

Then Gordon Sturgess, apparently intrigued by this clearly unexpected meeting between old acquaintances, put his oar in and said about the worst possible thing he could have done from Jardin's point of view. 'Ben lives hard by. Over in Buffalo Valley. He's a local man.'

'You don't say?' Roscoe drawled, getting to his feet now and turning away from his circle of companions—a fine-boned and well-proportioned six-footer, with the clear eye and long, hard muscles of the truly strong and enduring man. 'I must pay a call on him before long.'

'There's nothing for a man like you in

Buffalo Valley,' Jardin said dismissively, realizing he'd hastened that trifle too much. 'It's just a sodbuster's muckhole.'

'You keep a glass for an old friend there, don't you?'

'I keep a glass for any man who calls,' Jardin said. 'You never had much time for farms and farmers.'

'Never had much time for hard work,' Roscoe admitted. 'But I've got time for those who have.'

'Big of you, George,' Jardin observed dryly, feeling that the damage was now well and truly done. 'So come visiting if you like.'

'Mind if I bring my friends along too?'

'If they don't mind waiting outside.'

'That's not quite what I mean, Ben.'

'Ours isn't a big house,' Jardin explained, 'and we already have enough folk in it.'

'Hot damn!' Roscoe reflected. 'You Kansas farming folk are sort of tribal, aren't you? I'll bet you've got sisters.'

'In law.'

'Ben, that's not fair!' the barkeeper protested. 'What about your own kid sister? Young Emma is the toast of these parts—a real treat to look at.'

'Why don't you hold your row, Gordon?' Jardin asked as evenly as he could. 'Emma is a shy girl.'

'Doesn't like strangers, eh?' Roscoe questioned, his tones close and wicked. 'Is she afraid they might steal something from her? Her cherry, maybe?'

There was much haw-hawing at that. The men seated at the big round table began slapping each other on the back and winking at whomsoever caught their eye. Then they poured whisky from the bottles standing among them and toasted the very idea. Jardin considered them gravely, instinct warning him that the situation now stood on a knife-edge, and he took another swallow at his beer—inwardly cursing the need for pleasure which had brought him into the Hellgate saloon—then set his still half-filled mug aside. 'I've remembered,' he said, 'I've got some important business along the street. Must be off. Nice seeing you again, George.'

'Your business can wait,' Roscoe said

shortly. 'I want to hear some more about Emma. She sounds my kind of girl, Ben. I like 'em fresh as a daisy and full o' fighting spirit. Don't you remember?'

Jardin remembered all right. He remembered Atlanta, during Sherman's infamous march to the sea. Rape hadn't been in it, regardless of the military warning that Army rapists would be shot. Roscoe had been among the worst molesters of women—as indeed he had been among the worst of the looters and arsonists too—and Jardin realized that a man who could do such things in war could also do them in peace. He was sure that even now, sight unseen, Emma was under threat from Roscoe, and he knew that a stop had got to be put to it immediately. Whatever the cost! 'Forget anything I said before, Roscoe!' he cracked out. 'Stay away from Buffalo Valley! You'll find no welcome there!'

'What's that?' Roscoe demanded, face screwed up as if he couldn't believe his ears. 'You have the cheek?'

'Get the hell out!' Jardin warned, all

pretence at friendliness gone now and his tones deadly. 'We can do without you around Standish! At best, you and that bunch over there are up to no good! I can smell it!'

'Have you gone crazy?' Roscoe snarled.

'You heard me, mister!'

'You are crazy!' Roscoe gritted, striding closer to the man who was threatening him, his right hand moving towards his holster.

'Don't!' Jardin cautioned. 'When it comes to the shooting game, I'm better than you are. Always was—and I reckon you know it!'

'Maybe,' Roscoe said thickly. 'But I've got help, Ben. Every man sitting at that table is as good as you are.'

'I doubt it,' Jardin retorted. 'You never were one to surround yourself with your betters. Anyhow, I'll get you before they get me. Nothing will make you any the less dead!'

'We'll see,' Roscoe hissed—'we'll see.'

'No, we won't, dammit!' the barkeeper suddenly roared, heaving out an enormous shotgun from under the divide. 'There will be no gunfighting in here! If you two must have at it, you damned well do it in the back yard, like the pair of dogs you are!'

Jardin unbuckled his gunbelt. He slammed it down on top of the bar. Then, knowing that Roscoe—who gave no sign of divesting himself—would now use any dirty trick that he thought he could get away with, Jardin dived straight for the man, swinging a left hook as he went. The blow connected with the side of Roscoe's head. It spun him at the pace of a humming top towards one of the bar's big rear windows. Out through the glass the villain crashed, bright shards exploding around him, and he landed in the back yard and whirled to rest against the pump standing there with a considerable thud.

Simply bent on doing Roscoe all the harm he immediately could—and hoping that it would prove enough—Jardin sprang into the air and leapt out through the hole in the window left by the badman's body and, shedding further splinters of glass, he came to rest a few paces short of where

Roscoe lay. He lunged towards the other again, intending to heave him erect and deliver a finisher, but his stomach met a pair of quite unexpected boot-soles and the impact sent him staggering back against the rear wall of the saloon.

If proof of Roscoe's toughness had been needed, it was suddenly there; for, while the winded Jardin was still sucking air and collecting himself, the villain scrambled to his feet and came bounding in, punches flying. Quick of eye, Jardin would normally have fended off the blows without much difficulty, but he was in that moment a fraction slow and took a pair of hooks that set the spittle flying from his lips and the blood from his nose. Then an enormous thump to the belly doubled him up and a knee to the chin straightened him again just as quickly.

With senses revolving, Jardin spat out a tooth and some fragments of gum tissue. He heard the air bubbling in his bloody nostrils and found himself fighting to breathe. Chin tucked in and forearms and elbows blocking, he sought to absorb the

81

heaviest of the pounding while sustaining as little further real damage as possible, but too many of the badman's punches were getting through for all that and he felt his features swelling in a manner that he knew would render him partially blind before long. He just had to get away from Roscoe's threshing knuckles somehow; but, though he swayed and weaved, using all his natural skill to the utmost, the villain seemed to have him hemmed in, and there was little doubt that he would have succumbed to the barrage of blows if one of Roscoe's punches had not suddenly bounced off the side of his skull and then made further contact with serrated glass remains down an edge of the shattered window immediately to Jardin's rear and cut the knuckles of his right hand badly enough to cause him to cry out with pain and check for a moment.

Seizing his chance, Jardin shrank low, body circling at the hips, and dodged away to his left. Yet he realized how much slower he now was than his less battered adversary and perceived that his evasive action would not be enough in itself; so, thrusting his right leg behind Roscoe's right, he used the whole of his weight and what was left of his strength to shove his opponent off balance; and Roscoe went over even harder than he had hoped for and struck the back of his head on the ground hard enough to make his eyes start from their sockets. Roscoe lay there, limbs flexing in a weakness which their owner could no more than half control and, grabbing the man by his shirtfront before he could make any degree of fuller recovery, Jardin jerked his torso off the ground and thumped over a left cross, the blow turning Roscoe's head dangerously far on a spine that ridged visibly at the back of his neck.

Repeating the dose with hardly less force, Jardin flattened his enemy completely. He believed that the other was unconscious and the fight won; but, as he straightend up and tipped back his chin to breathe, Roscoe—who was still in possession of his revolver—moved his bleeding right hand unexpectedly and fumbled his weapon out, clearly intending to shoot the man who loomed above him.

Jardin kicked out with all his force. The toe of his boot went in true and ripped the pistol out of Roscoe's grasp, propelling the Colt into the rear of the yard, where it clattered down far beyond its owner's reach. Appearing to realize that his last chance for any kind of victory had been snatched from him, Roscoe gave in to rage and fear. He came off the ground, visibly shaking himself together, and essayed a dive at Jardin's legs; but, watching the lunge of the other's jaw at the level of his own waist, Jardin pumped his right knee upwards again and once more brought it into contact with his adversary's jaw. Roscoe hit the ground again, flung full length, and this time he lay absolutely inert. Indeed, he showed no sign of stirring again—perhaps ever.

Jardin stepped back. A door in the rear wall of the saloon burst open and men came tumbling out into the yard. Jardin could see that they were Roscoe's friends, but he made no attempt to run from them, knowing that rough men had a great respect for physical combat and almost never turned on the winner of a good fight. So it was now, and the men from the big round table by-passed him and went at once to where Roscoe lay. They formed a circle around his motionless figure and began nid-nodding, and a number of seconds went by before a long, bent-shouldered man, with the arms of an ape, a hare-lip, and a dark, leery eye above a steep-sunburned nose, screwed his doghead round and said in lilting Southern accents that didn't somehow match the rest of him: 'Shuah looks like you done gone and killed him, boy.'

'Not a blasted chance!' Jardin scoffed thickly. 'It'd take more than a knee in the face to kill a bastard like him!'

'The man's right, Jockey,' a shorter but far more heavily built member of the company informed the taller fellow. 'Look, will you! His nostrils is a-twitchin'.'

'Well, that's good, ain't it, Tompkin?' Jockey inquired. 'You want him dead or somethin'?'

'More like you do, Dunn!' Tompkin jeered. 'That'd make you top man!'

'Ow?' Jockey Dunn mocked in his turn. 'What's so special about bein' the boss then?'

'You git the boss's cut, that's what.'

'You-all figger that's so much o'late, Lew?' Dunn inquired. ''Tain't no big concern with me.'

'And you're a liar!' Tompkin spat.

'Supposin' you two hold your silly rows?' an older man suggested, turning a gap-toothed, razor-scarred face that had been weathered teak-hard by half a lifetime spent in sun, storm, and freezing cold. 'If one of you wants to make himself some use, how about fetching a bucket and pumping out some water? Whatever Roscoe is or ain't, he's our man, and I dare swear he ain't going to be worth a plugged nickel to us when he pulls round.'

'Don't you start that again, Oily Bowes!' Tompkin warned, shaking a finger in the older man's face. 'We don't need no c'rection from your likes. I've got tired o' that sharp-shootin' jaw o' your just lately!'

86

'If there's a guy in this party who'd like to take George Roscoe's place, Lew,' Olly Bowes said fearlessly, 'it's you. As for the rewards, they've gotta be earned. But they'll come. We're in the right street again up here.'

'Now that shuah is talk we c'n do without, Mr Bowes,' Jockey Dunn said warningly. 'You want the world and his wife to hear you runnin' off at the lip? 'Low you're right about that water though. How if you see t'gittin' it?'

'All right,' Bowes said co-operatively enough. 'All right, my man.'

Jardin watched Bowes start poking about the yard, presumably in search of a bucket, then decided that he had seen and heard enough of this suspect crew. Turning away, he more dragged himself than walked through the door that the erupting men had opened up on his left and made for the bar, where Gordon Sturgess was once more polishing a glass. The barkeeper's enormous shotgun had been put out of sight again and a hush now lay upon the bar-room, for the chuck-a-luck wheel had stopped turning and the other forms of gambling also ceased. 'Sorry, Gordon,' Jardin said, picking up his gunbelt from where he had left it on top of the bar and swinging it about his waist. 'It had to be. In the end I didn't have a choice.'

'Sure,' Sturgess said reluctantly. 'I guess I said the wrong things.'

'You didn't help,' Jardin commented, latching up, spitting blood into a spittoon, then dashing away the clotted redness from beneath his injured nostrils—'and that's a fact.'

'I don't want to hear any more about it,' the barkeeper said sternly. 'You ran out the winner, and I'll probably be paying for the damage.'

'Better than bringing the law into it,' Jardin said, paying Sturgess back for his lack of sympathy. Then he studied himself disgustedly in the backbar mirror. 'What a sight!'

'You sure are a mess, Ben,' Sturgess agreed. 'You'll never live it down if you go home like that.'

'I fear you're right,' Jardin admitted,

spitting blood again from where he had lost the tooth. 'What do you think I should do?'

'Don't go home for a day or two. Take a room along the street. Try the Widness boarding house for preference. Ivy isn't too fussy about who she has there.'

'That sounds nice!'

'Who the dickens are you to complain?' the barkeeper inquired ironically.

'Reckon you're right,' Jardin growled.

'Be off, Ben—before those guys out there bring that dirty-minded pal of theirs back in here!'

Jardin managed a curt little nod. Facing away from the bar, he lurched out through the batwings and into the street. Feeling as if he were walking on cotton waste, he went to his horse and freed it from the hitching rail. Then he caught the animal at the bit and began walking it northwards, much too ill to climb into the saddle. Repeatedly spitting and sniffing amidst the bloody misery of his hurts, Jardin simply kept putting one foot in front of the other and left Ma Widness's boarding house behind him on the left—because he knew that even the tolerance of the rough-and-ready Ivy wouldn't extend to his present condition—and he cleared town and turned off the trail beyond it, heading a short distance into the country west of Standish and coming soon to the small lake in which he had often fished as a kid.

Here he went to his favourite bay, a green and sheltered place, and tied his horse into a bush. Then he lowered himself onto his belly at the water's-edge and sank his bruised hands into the lake's cold, clear liquid, doing the same with his face thereafter and coming up for air only as often as he found necessary.

Later on, when his bruised cheeks and split nostrils felt soothed, he stripped off and stepped into the water, floating there for an hour and more until the dark blotches on his stomach and chest were likewise eased. After that he hauled himself back onto the bank and lay naked in the sun, drying off by degrees and relaxing in the same measure. By mid-afternoon he was no longer bleeding anywhere and his brain had cleared. By now he was fairly sure, too, that he was not badly hurt—and that his only real loss was the sound tooth which he had been forced to spit away—but fights reaching the violence which the one between him and George Roscoe had achieved almost invariably left some damage to the body that couldn't be made good. Altogether, he had been lucky, and he hoped that he would never have to fight another battle like the one at the Hellgate saloon as long as he lived.

Presently, lulled by the warmth of the afternoon, Jardin slept for an hour or two, and the early evening had arrived before he awakened sufficiently to pull on his clothes again and think about getting back to town and hiring a room for the night at the Widness boarding house. Yawning, he once more freed his horse; then, leading it clear of the lakeside greenery, found that he was able to swing up without much difficulty and ride comfortably enough.

He headed back for the trail, slanting off to the right with a view to cutting the track north about a hundred yards short of where

Standish's main street began. The ground in this direction was a little more rugged than that over which he had walked to the lakeside so many hours earlier in the day, and he spurred his mount over the grassy undulations with an urgency that belied his true indifference to most things about then; and he was getting ready to top out with a final surge off the spur after a brief but steepish climb, when he heard the hollered conversation of several men from somewhere not too far ahead of him.

Judging that he must be closer to the trail than he'd thought—since he deemed the talk to be that of riders—Jardin caught at his reins, checking his horse sufficiently to bring its head over the ridge above at about a sixth of the speed that he had originally intended. Now he halted the brute—not too squarely braced but nevertheless safely grounded—and lifted carefully out of his seat, standing in his stirrups to peer over the crest and across the land beyond. About eighty yards away and on the trail that ran northwards out of

Standish, he saw riding the group of men whom he had encountered that morning in the Hellgate saloon. Led by George Roscoe, who was travelling hatless and had a flavour of drunken bravado about him, they were cantering up country and seemed to be trying to urge a slower pace on their leader, but he in his turn was shouting back slurred words of encouragement to his followers that appeared to be exhorting haste. Jardin listened intently, and twice the phrase 'the big herd' carried clearly to him, though little else was in any sense plain; and, as the calling voices receded, the listener was left with no clear idea of what the noisy disputation had been about.

Still Jardin watched. The riders went onwards, and soon they were well up the trail. Then they passed from sight into a dip about a quarter of a mile away. Striking with his heels again, Jardin forced his horse across the ridge and resumed heading for the trail. On reaching it, he bent right and made for the Standish limits, for these were visible just the short distance ahead that he had expected.

There was a new uneasiness in Jardin as he re-entered town. Strangely enough, it wasn't so much for himself that he feared as others. He had a strong feeling that there was major wickedness afoot, and that he, through George Roscoe, was somehow connected with it. If only he had a clearer insight into what threatened. But perhaps that would come—and he would then wish it away.

FIVE

Jardin spent an uncomfortable night on the thin mattress of his boarding house bed. Because of this, he didn't get off to sleep before the early hours and awakened later than he had intended the next morning. On getting out of bed, he discovered that he hurt in many places which had not been sore the day before, and it was only by an act of will that he contrived to pull his shirt and pants on and then stagger over to the washstand and have a rinse. After that he moved stiffly to the chest-of-drawers and looked into the glass on top of it, combing his hair with his fingers as he studied the wan and disfigured state of his face. Yet bad as he looked, he didn't look even half as bad as he had the day before, since yesterday's long immersion in cold water had undoubtedly reduced the swelling in his features and washed away all trace of congealed blood from his split nostrils. A still battered-looking man, he reckoned that he was just about passable in average company and, on the strength of that, he stamped into his boots and more or less shambled downstairs, entering Ivy Widness's communal dining room and asking for breakfast.

He ate his eggs and bacon in a state of brown study. His mind had cooled down overnight, and the feverish anxiety which had troubled him on the way here yesterday evening had reduced to a kind of ominous shadow that lurked at the back of his mind. But it was still an influential presence there, and he could not ignore it, since he knew himself for a highly intuitive man who was seldom completely wrong when he felt that there was trouble about. That phrase which he had twice heard from George Roscoe's lips—while it could allude to many things and have as many applications—kept bringing his mind to Tom Tupper and the Texas herd that he had seen heading towards the Blue Grass Valley a trifle over twenty-four hours ago. 'That big herd' of the quotation could well be Tupper's herd—particularly as the trail-boss's bovine charges were said to be the only mass of Southern cows presently around—and Tupper and his outfit could quite possibly be under some kind of threat from Roscoe and that unsavoury bunch he was bossing. There had been that ill-omened talk among the hardcases—while Roscoe had lain unconscious in the Hallgate saloon's back yard—about rewards having to be earned and the men being in the right street for that again. It all fitted sure enough, and the atmosphere of graft clung to it.

Conscience kept prodding at Jardin. He ought to do something. It was all very well to sit here feeding his face, when Tupper and company could be under threat, but he'd never forgive himself if some tragic event that he could have averted overtook the Texans. His obvious move was to visit the sheriff, of course; but, though his suspicions made sense to him, what did he really have to go on that was likely to spur the law into action? Precious little, when it came right down to it. There was Roscoe's character as a whole, the things the man had done during the war, the crimes that folk always associated with the kind of bunch that he was currently heading, and the admittedly ambiguous phrase which he had twice uttered. If you put the lot together, you lacked enough to make the common run of lawman prick up his ears. You could be sure that Sheriff Abe Holst wasn't going to hunt trouble, and that he would howl as loudly as the next of his breed that more than enough of it came to him of its own accord. No, this had to remain a private affair—a problem of judgment no less than conscience—and Jardin realized that whatever he did would have to be done in light of the reasons that he had already set out. If he acted and proved wrong, he would have to suffer the mockery of it, yet if he didn't act and proved right—Ah, there indeed was the rub! But he didn't absolutely have to stake his peace of mind on either course. Who else knew what he knew? And who was to step up and blame him if he simply slipped away into the distance again and let anything happen that was going to happen—or not, as the matter turned out?

Jardin rose from his chair abruptly, tongue probing irritably at the foul-tasting hole from which he had lost that tooth yesterday, and he knew that he must ride out and overtake the Tupper herd or he would never know an hour's rest again.

Leaving the dining room, he went through the house and found the vinegary, faded Mrs Widness, with her steel-rimmed glasses and grey bun, and paid her what he owed for his bed and breakfast. Then he walked outside and over to the hitching rail at which his horse was standing. Breaking the brute's tie with a decisive jerk, he stepped up and and trotted the mount northwards, heels striking as he cleared the limits and working the horse up to a gallop.

He followed the trail up country for a bit over a mile, then angled away to the left, pounding over bunch-grass now and heading for a roughly plotted point about five miles to the northwest or where he and the beaten way had just parted company. For the first time since he had left the Hellgate saloon yesterday, he felt something like himself again, and he hoped a long gallop would free his remaining adhesions and make him at least ninety percent of the man he normally was; but this was another of those worthy intentions doomed to go awry, for he had not covered another mile when he saw, a short way ahead of him and directly crossing his path, a rider who was slumped in a bloody saddle and obviously carrying lead.

Slowing, Jardin eased over to the right

and approached the wounded horseman at a checked canter, halting his own and the other's slow-moving mount with such pressure as was necessary on either hand. He was already aware that the fellow on the horse opposite was little more than a youth, and he gripped the shot man's bronze quiff and tipped his drooping head backwards, fearing the worst, but he perceived at once that the young man had received a wound from which he would be unlikely to die, providing he received proper care. The bullet had hit him just below the left shoulder—at a spot, indeed, where the lung had been missed and the collar-bone too—and the kid was still fully aware of what was happening and showed a flash of humour as he rolled a blue eye and drawled: 'Can't you let a fellow doze?'

'Ding-dong, boy!' Jardin snorted. 'Wake yourself up! There's a day's work ahead!'

'When wasn't there?' the boy complained.

'Oh, to hell with it!' Jardin growled compassionately. 'You're hurt bad enough.

What's your name?'

'Jim Lyons.'

'You one of Tupper's boys?' Jardin hazarded.

'Last I heard.'

'What happened?' Jardin asked. 'I mean, Jim, did it just happen to you?'

'No, it was them guys,' Lyons explained. 'Nine or ten of 'em there were—ugly customers. Just after sunup, when we'd just got the herd movin' again—they stopped us.'

'Go on,' Jardin insisted, feeling that he had better get whatever was here out of the kid while Lyons was still up to it.

'They said they were herd-cutters,' the youngster went on, swallowing. 'The official herd-cutters for the district. Tupper told 'em he hadn't heard of any such body, but the guy in charge o' that bunch declared it was so. He reckoned they were goin' to cut that blasted herd of ours whether Tom liked it or not. So Tom, being the easy man he mostly is, said they'd better get on with it, and they did.'

'Uh, huh?' Jardin prompted, helping the hurt youngster to keep his seat.

'Those men found critters the herd had swept up all right. A lot of them.'

'Well, that's normal,' Jardin observed. 'How are you to account for some of the other man's cows getting mixed up with yours? It's a problem natural to a cattle drive. Okay—so they cut 'em out. What then?'

'They started cuttin' out beasts that carried our Texas brands,' Lyons answered. 'At first Tupper figured they were makin' some kind of mistake, but it went on—brazen as you like—and it weren't long before them hellions had roped in about a hundred and fifty head which they aimed to drive off wheresoever, half o' them beasts being legitimate Texas stock and not reared any place else.'

'No human being could let that go, Jim,' Jardin reflected. 'Tupper protested?'

'Sure,' Lyons acknowledged—'and one of our clowns went and jerked a six-shooter.'

'Oh, my God!' Jardin breathed. 'I can

see it all too clearly. They'd have shot that man on the spot, and the rest of you would just naturally have gone for your guns.'

'You've got it,' Lyons agreed. 'That's just what happened. Only we weren't up to it. If you ask me, that bunch are professional gunslingers to a man. They shot us down before we hardly knew what had hit us. I was being covered out on the herd's right wing, and was among the first to stop a slug, but I reckon it was just that saved me, 'cos my horse faced round from the gunflashes where the battle was hot and dashed off into the herd—which was millin', climbin' and a-stampedin', and all sorts by then—and eventually I kinda slunk out of the ruck and let my nag carry me into some trees. It figures them herd-cutters didn't see me going, 'cos I wasn't chased any, though I will allow I was beginnin' to lose count of things when you pulled me up.'

'It's a wrong 'un all right,' Jardin commented. 'I think I know who those herd-cutters are, and I dare swear they're no appointed body, but I can't right out prove it, Jim. The name of that leader you spoke of is likely George Roscoe, and he is the soul of evil, boy! Trouble is, if the herd-cutters are official—and you admit your side started the actual gunplay—I reckon that puts you Texans in the wrong, whatever the real truth behind it may be.'

'What're you bitin' on, mister?' Lyons queried.

'I'm Ben Jardin, boy,' Jardin said, smiling bitterly to himself; for, with all that he had just heard, he remained in precisely the same position which he had been in earlier on. 'And I mean I can't go spouting to the law until I'm exactly sure of what I'm spouting about. Not that I'm struck on the law at the best of the times, but it's there and we've got to keep its commandments. Because that's what being a good citizen is all about.'

'If you say so, Mr Jardin.'

'I do,' Jardin responded. 'And I'll thank you not to take the Irish.'

'You're such an old sobersides,' Lyons complained.

'That before you even know me!' Jardin snorted, turning his head south of east and gazing across the land. 'Jim, I can't take you into town—without risking an uproar that I reckon we can both do without for now. So I'm going to take you home with me. I've got folk there who I think can take good care of you. If there's a real need to get the doctor in, I'll do it myself. But, on giving you a close look, it appears to me that bullet went clear through you. That being so, it's just a matter of binding you up clean and keeping infection out. You're young, healthy, and should heal fast.'

'I'm in no shape to give you an argument,' Lyons said faintly. 'How far to your home?'

'Six or seven miles,' Jardin answered. 'It isn't that far. Do you think you can make it in your saddle—if we ride slow?'

'If we ride slow, yes.'

Doubtful about all of it—though believing that he was going to act for the best—Jardin withdrew his direct support from the wounded youngster and watched carefully as Lyons straightened his back and put a bracing hand on the cap of his high Texas pommel, gazing before him then with swimmy, pain-filled eyes that were nevertheless resolute. The kid's mouth was flattened too, and it was already plain that he was going to be a tough one in his day—the sort who would only give up when life or his senses left him. 'You'll do,' Jardin said. 'Hang on, and you'll be lying on a soft bed an hour or so from now.'

'I hear you, Mr Jardin.'

'Ben will do.'

'I hear you even better now—Ben.'

'You sassy young pup!' Jardin chuckled. 'Come on. Give that cayuse a prod!'

Lyons stirred his horse into motion. Riding close in at the kid's side, Jardin intimated their course at intervals, and they rode across the empty plain which flowed beneath the quarter of the sky that the sun would soon be leaving. The younger man stuck it very well, making almost no murmur, and they steadily reeled in the miles, eventually arriving at the northern exit of Buffalo Valley. Here they turned southwards into the valley and then rode down the greater part of its length, finally reaching the Jardin farm and reining in near the front door of the house. Now the older man gave his wounded charge a nod of approval and said: 'Nicely.'

The front door of the dwelling opened abruptly and young Emma Jardin stepped out. Her face was flushed with indignation, and she jammed her fists into the sides of her waist and snapped: 'Ben, we've been worried about you! Where did you get to last night?'

'You should know better than to worry about me,' Jardin said shortly. 'I come and go as I have to.'

'You've been fighting,' Emma accused, her eyes mainly on Jim Lyons now, as they really had been from the start. 'You're a sight!' She stepped up closer to Jim Lyons' horse. 'Who is he, Ben? He's covered in blood!'

'He's a Texas trailherder,' Jardin replied. 'One of Tom Tupper's men. He's been shot.'

'I can see that,' Emma said. 'Why have you brought him here? Town is the right place for him. The doctor's house.'

'I'll call in Max Friend if I have to, Emma,' Jardin said. 'It didn't suit me to take him into town. I had my own reasons—good ones. As for the rest, I'm pretty sure the bullet passed through his body. That should mean he needs only bandaging and bedrest. We should be able to do that much for him without straining ourselves.'

'More work for the women.'

'There are three of you,' Jardin reminded.

'Where are you going to be?'

'Once I've seen him into bed,' Jardin said, 'I've other matters to look into. I shan't be here.'

'Ben,' the girl sighed, 'you're never at home these days. Will it do any good to pry?'

'None at all,' he assured her, dismounting now, going to Lyons' horse, and lifting the young man down into his arms. 'Okay boy?'

'Hate to be a trouble,' the other whispered. 'My head's going round.'

'Shock and loss of blood,' Jardin said, raising his eyebrows at his sister. 'His name is Jim—Jim Lyons—and he's all yours.'

'From Texas, ma'am,' Lyons said, his whisper reduced to a mutter. 'Hate to be a—'

'He's passing out, Ben,' Emma said.

'I can see,' her brother returned. 'Step inside, girl, and I'll carry him indoors behind you.'

Emma obeyed. Then Jardin steered his burden into the house. He crossed the living room and, laying the newly fainted Lyons on the dining table that Emma had just cleared for him with a sweep at the cloth, began at once pulling the waist of the young Texans's shirt out of his trousers as the first act of undressing him.

'What *is* this all about?' Emma pleaded, making a slight face and gazing rather tentatively at the blue-edged bullet-hole just beneath the trailherder's left shoulder. 'I don't want to put my nose—'

'Then don't,' Jardin interrupted firmly.

'Oh, Ben!' Emma snapped rebelliously. 'I must!'

'I can't tell you anything,' Jardin responded. 'I don't know much for sure myself. There's something happening around here—I believe—that could be worse than anything we've ever known. The only other thing I can say is that, if I've been told aright, this boy is real lucky to be alive.'

'Does this have anything to do with what happened to Sam Carter?'

'That's a big jump, Emma,' he commented, whistling just audibly to himself. 'It seems crazy to even think that it could. Yet it just might do. 'Pears to me, there's always a marrying up between the big events somewhere.'

'And that's all you've got to say?'

Jardin drew the trousers off Jim Lyons and left him lying there in his long underwear. Then he raised the young man's torso, looking down the Texan's back for any rear view of the bullet wound, and he saw that the slug had not only passed right through but had done so cleanly. Now, nodding his satisfaction, he said: 'Hot water and some bandages. I

110

figure if these holes are bathed clean, then bound up, Jim Lyons will be good as new in a few days.'

'Why don't you leave him to me?' Emma asked shortly. 'I can see you're on the jiffle to be off again. Brothers Joe and Harry can help me get this boy to bed. I'll call them in from the land when I need them.'

'Thank you, sis,' Jardin said, happy to avail himself of what she suggested. 'That's a good idea of yours. You can't beat the woman's touch. I'll be on my way then. If I'm not home again tonight, don't think anything of it. This matters, Emma.'

'Ben,' the girl said anxiously, 'don't get too full of yourself. There's plenty going on in Kansas today, both for good and ill, that's no concern of yours. Be careful where you stick *your* nose in.'

Jardin turned his head and blinked at her. He was jolted despite himself, for he appreciated that an unexamined feeling of self-importance could—often deservedly—land a man in a lot of trouble. Yet what Emma had just said—and had probably felt needed to be said on the spur of the moment—was true only when a man was interfering in legitimate affairs. Where law-breaking was concerned, whatever the form it took, every citizen had the right to question and intrude—though, of course, at his own risk—and he suspected that it had been more in fear for his hide than in a genuine spirit of admonishment that Emma had spoken. Knowing him for a reasonably modest man, she had simply been using his own nature against him in an effort to divert him. At that, he didn't amount to much, with his rough ways and lack of education, but he was nevertheless genuinely strong for the right and felt that he had got to go on so being. An element of secrecy could be important to what he intended—and he felt that strongly—yet he said with a certain humility: 'Okay, Emma. I'm riding to the ground north of Blue Grass Valley. A herd-cutting went wrong over there. I'm pretty sure I know the man responsible, and I can't believe it's the official job he claims. It's most likely Jim Lyons is the only survivor of Tom Tupper's outfit, and I want to find out what's become of the herd those Texans were driving. Whatever happens, you just can't dispose of all those cows willy-nilly, and responsibility must out. I figure a big crime has been committed, and that local folk—inbred to a pack of thieves—could be involved.'

'Go to the sheriff, Ben,' Emma urged.

'Can't until I'm certain there has been wrongdoing.'

'You can too!' Emma insisted, her right foot stamping.

Jardin departed on those words, and rode away from the house up valley with their import dinning through his head. As he gazed northwards, into the sunless tumble of a cloudy sky, he knew she was right and that didn't sit too well with him, since she *was* only nineteen. It was all very well to describe her as the wise one of the family in circumstances that titillated the Jardin pride, but he was supposed to be the head of the family and the man to whom everybody looked for sound reasoning in the broadest sense. Altogether, he could now perceive that he had not been reasoning soundly here. At best, a tragic incident had occurred and the law ought to learn of it without delay. In this matter he could neither make a fool of himself nor adversely influence other aspects of his affairs. More, he had at home a witness for the dead as to what had actually occurred between the herd-cutters and Tupper's drovers, so he could himself be said to be the prime witness after the fact, even if no provable crime had been committed beyond Blue Grass Valley. Thus he could with impunity rid himself of the responsibility for playing either a detective or a snoop—and the law might even honour him for it—but the fact was that some rather obscure mental thread, already hinted at in the faint possibility that Sam Carter's murder could be connected with this morning's shoot-out between the herd-cutters and the Texas drovers, held him to his desire to seek the truth for himself and accept the likely risks that could entail. But the danger also lured and excited, and there perhaps was the true weakness in his pose—rather than role—as the responsible citizen.

Speeding up a bit, Jardin cleared the northern end of Buffalo Valley and slanted to the left, riding the same grass again over which he had brought the wounded Jim Lyons earlier on. Seeing no reason why he should cause his own impatience to punish his horse, he held to the steady gallop that he had set up back in the valley and aimed for the spot where he had first come across Lyons. Reaching it, he tightened his angle of travel a little to the south and went on riding much as before, only slowing down when he saw dust rising a mile or two ahead of him and realized that this must indicate that Tupper's herd had been turned from its original course and was now being driven almost due west into land that was almost certainly owned by Dave Harper, master of the Box H.

Jardin recognised that this could be significant, yet knew that it might also mean no more than that the herd-cutters were driving the Tupper herd into land where the cows could feed temporarily without impeding any other herd that might come in this direction. With his inner vision subdued, and little detail clogging his will to pursue, Jardin swung away into country that would carry him down the left wing of the herd, providing that the drovers forced no change of course in the next mile or two, and simply nursed his curiosity as he went along. For, though he was a local man, there was a lot of country about here that he didn't know intimately, so the possible destination of the re-routed herd was not one that he could readily anticipate. But, as a roughly diamond-shaped pattern of knolls rose out of the land immediately ahead, he at once recalled a large depression among the hillocks and reckoned that this was the likely place to which the herd was being pushed. With the waterhole that he now also remembered at the hollow's centre, the need of the cows for grass and liquid would be fully met in the short term, and it would also be relatively easy for a handful of men to ride the containing rim and hold the likewise concealed herd in place. Yes, that must be it.

Coming level with the herd, Jardin let himself drift along as it drifted, while making sure that he kept below the land wherever he could, and the driven beasts were nearing the ground within the diamond-shape—and he was thinking of galloping to the back of the area and ascending the most westerly of the hillocks, to get a view of the hollow's filling from the best height he could achieve—when he heard a shout from behind him and realized that his shadowing presence had been spotted by men other than the herders themselves. Cursing his failure to be vigilant on all sides, Jardin instantly admitted his furtive designs by spurring for full gallop, and within the moment he heard somebody yell: 'Get after him him! No guns, dammit! We can sure do without a new stampede on our hands!'

There was, then, that much to be thankful for.

SIX

Jardin got his head down and went at it, heels digging. He covered more than half a mile before risking a glance to his rear. Then, on a stretch of level going, he craned and gazed back along his tracks. What he beheld rather dismayed him; for, on the evidence of his ears earlier, he had estimated that he had commenced his flight at least a couple of hundred yards up on his pursuers—and he had believed that his instant dive for the distance would have increased his lead rather than the reverse—but now he saw that of the four men he counted in his wake, one was less than a hundred and fifty yards back and closing on him steadily.

Knowing that he stood a good chance of being overtaken and pulled from his saddle very shortly, Jardin did what he invariably did in times of emergency and let his instinct take over. Then, reacting to the prompt response of his subconscious mind, he drew to the right and veered away from what had become the settled line of the chase. Now he began climbing a suitable part of the inclined circle of land which enclosed the big depression nearby, horse tucking its rear legs hard as it heaved its way upwards.

He topped out, noting the lather that had appeared along his mount's flanks, but judging that, in more normal circumstances, the men behind him would have put a bullet in his back long ago. It was as well that they had obeyed the command to refrain from shooting and remained no more than chasing riders. That had unquestionably kept him alive and preserved what slight measure of advantage was still with him. Now he sent his horse stretching downhill and into the low, then out across the noses of the cows surging towards the centre of the hollow down the long and fairly shallow slope on his right. It was a close thing. As he went along, he was often forced to dodge through the scattering of faster cows that formed the herd's vanguard. Yet he knew, without looking back, that the riders behind him were going to arrive at his essential starting point too late to follow his example on this lower level. They were going to find themselves perhaps totally checked by the mass of bovine rushing downwards on their right. Reaching the northern wall, Jardin began to climb again, wondering if his pursuers would have the sense—and fearing that they probably had as much as he—to turn left before making contact with the onrush and then outrun the herd down to the depression's middle. For after that they could swing around the base of the hollow and gallop to the northern wall of the low, where it would be easy to climb into his tracks again and resume the chase.

But all that was for the next stage of the pursuit—if it manifested at all—and Jardin was content to keep pounding onwards and upwards in the sure knowledge that he had at least temporarily outwitted his hunters and must certainly have extended his lead by a lot.

It seemed to him that he arrived on the northern rim of the hollow quite suddenly. Here he allowed himself the full glance back that he had been so anxious to take for the last minute or two. He saw that he had done even better than he had hoped. For his pursuers had evidently been little more than slowed on meeting the front of the herd initially and tried to thread or battle through the leading ranks; but, from their position now in the mass below, the sheer weight of the descending beeves must have finally compelled them to turn into the herd and travel with it down to the middle of the hollow. Currently, his hunters were disentangling themselves from among the jostling beasts and gesticulating the routes that different riders could follow round to the foot of the climb that he had already completed.

Yes, it looked pretty good for him back there and Jardin put his horse to the new descent before him confidently. He let the brute lunge and slither towards the plain below and, reaching it, swung left and wide for the back of the hillock that he had recently planned to climb at the point to the extreme west of the area. There seemed nothing to it now, and he would have made a clean getaway there and then—since his pursuers should have had no chance to spot the direction which he had taken on the lower grass—but he was still riding his sister Emma's ageing Buck and the pace was starting to tell on the now heavily sweating animal, which showed signs of failing altogether if he pushed it to the limit for too much longer.

The energies of the horse had to be conserved. Gambling that his hunters would still not top out behind him before he had got out of sight, Jardin slowed appreciably but kept following the same course. He reached the shadow of the hillock those seconds later than would previously have been the case and, peering worriedly over his left shoulder, prayed that the northern crest of the hollow would remain as empty as it was just then until he had passed fully under the land; but, as with Satan's own luck, his pursuers surged into view just before the mass of the knoll claimed him and the loud shout which immediately went up told him that he had been spotted once more and the chase was still on.

Jardin released a pent up breath, forehead creasing. It seemed that fortune had deserted him, yet matters could be worse. His lead over the men on the higher ground was more than half a mile, and their horses could well have received a buffeting from the herd that had taken plenty out of them. He talked to the brute under him, flattering and cajoling most of the time—since the old gelding liked that—and the mount held to a steady pace and rounded the side of the hillock, rougher land now appearing off another decline and about three-quarters of a mile ahead.

If the circumstances had been more propitious, Jardin would have avoided those gullies and benches as dangerous ground onto which to take a tired horse; but now he headed straight for them, figuring that if he could not outrun his pursuers, he might be able to hide from them where the rock-piles tumbled and thickets were plentiful. So he let his mount stretch and tuck in the old familiar rhythm as it crossed the gently dipping grass before them and aimed for a spot under the benches that appeared to provide a good take-off into an easy climb that ought to carry them without much strain on man or beast into the boulder-heaps which disfigured the slightly rearing skyline of the immediate west.

Nearing the ascent, Jardin again looked back. He could not see his hunters on the land behind him but, having traversed the brief stretch of plain between him and the nearby hillock for himself, he thought it likely that they could see him out of the gloom that ringed the base of the slight eminence and had to assume that this stage of his flight was also an open book for them to read as they wished. Not that that daunted him a lot, for he was dealing with the obvious just now and realized that no trick he could devise in the immediate situation would be likely to throw the pursuit off anyhow. The presence of the men behind him was inevitable while they had him in sight—and he was sure that they were confident they had his intentions weighed up for the minute—but it was on this matter-of-fact certainty that he was going to pin his hopes, for the average manhunter did not expect a quarry who had been in full view for a good while to attempt something audacious the instant that he got out of it. The average mind was not prone to sudden adjustments unless previously alerted, and the natural instinct for a pursuer—partially hypnotised by the running experience—was to expect the pursued to go on fleeing for a while once out of sight; so, when evasive action was taken in these circumstances, more or less at a snap of the fingers, the follower was frequently caught off guard. Or so Jardin had often seen it, and he had found his experience reliable in most things.

Jardin deliberately relaxed and let his horse enter the climb ahead in its own fashion. With only the least pressure from its rider's slightly inclined body remaining, the animal reached and scrambled over the broad ledges of the slope, as sure-footed as a colt. Carefully avoiding the thickets of dogwood and willow, as any horseman would, Jardin let it all seem to happen naturally, leaving himself in full view among the upper rock-piles until he had even convinced himself that he must be going over the ridge within moments and down into whatever country extended beyond. Then, just below the very top itself, he veered to the right and put a rock mass which had long suggested itself as meeting his needs between him and the eyes that he had no doubt were watching from the grass in his wake. After that, praying that his hunters had been deceived by his abrupt disappearance and believed that he had in fact crossed the ridge, he passed round the top and down the further side of the stone bulk that was hiding him. Then he descended a few yards more and ended up behind a thicket of blackthorn, ash, and scrub oak.

Holding his horse completely still, Jardin sat as lightly as he could and nerved himself to wait, ears straining though every other part of his body was loose. Loud talk was audible for a moment as the pursuers reached the foot of the roughly stepped grade on which their quarry was hiding, but the delay between the burst of conversation and the riders climbing to the level of Jardin's concealment seemed interminable—though a minute or so probably covered it—and the fugitive found that he had assimilated the worst of his apprehension and was left cold as the riders passed opposite and then crossed the ridge behind him without pause or the smallest suspicious word. He could hardly credit that it had been so very easy and, though he held his position for a short while longer—to make sure that the hunters had ridden on far enough to hear nothing of whatever movements he made on this side of the ridge—he was reasonably certain that his extra care was wasted and that he could have left his hiding place and descended to the grass again almost straightaway. His pursuers hadn't had the ghost of a notion that they had been tricked in the simplest of manners, and Jardin felt little respect for them.

Plucking and nudging at his mount, Jardin eased away from the thicket which had hidden him from view and then rode downwards. Regaining the graze below without mishap, he turned right along the base of the terraced slope beside him and peered into the south, seeing there a small, dark-looking wood. Considering the timber, he thought it would make an ideal curtain to put between him and the eventual return of his hunters, and he reckoned that he would ride over there and pass through it while everything was still in his favour. There was, he also saw, a fold in the plain nearby that came within a short distance at either end of linking this present ground and the wood. Thankful for this piece of improved fortune—since the tuck in the earth's surface would hide his next movements from almost any eyes that happened to be around—he spurred onwards and rode down into the fold, following its sunken length after that until a short climb brought him out of the vanishing crease close to the pine trees that formed a loose and often sparse fringe along the wood's western limits.

Still riding along at a good pace, Jardin was preparing to duck his head and enter the trees—a greater fall of light beyond the sun-flecked gloom that he could already see in the middle timber drawing him towards the land on the eastern side of the wood—when a loud metallic squeak that he could not at once identify almost made him jump out of his skin and saddle alike. Gaze turning towards the spot from which the noise had come, he made out a farm waggon standing behind a large mass of hanging foliage a few yards to his right. The vehicle obviously had its brake off, and the erratic jerking movements of the cropping horse between its shafts were producing frequent repeats of the shrill squeaking sound from some ungreased moving part of its structure.

The presence of the horse and cart clearly meant that there was somebody around, and this in turn meant that Jardin could again be in danger of discovery.

Certainly he must not ride through the wood as openly as he had planned; so, reining in, he dismounted and stood looking uncertainly around him. Then, from somewhere not too far off in the trees adjacent, he heard what sounded like a pick thudding and two men engaged in a faintly querulous conversation, no word of which was intelligible to him at this range. Calculating, he judged that the sounds of work and talk were coming from his right and about thirty yards into the wood. Thus, if he moved out to his far left and stayed afoot, leading his horse, he should be able to by-pass the men and their activity with almost no risk of being seen or heard. This, of course, was mainly what he wanted, yet he sensed something peculiar about the unseen doings and his curiosity was aroused.

Almost despite himself, Jardin felt drawn to see what was going on; and, after leading his horse behind an evergreen bush and tethering it there, he snaked over to the cart and had a quick look in its back, but he saw nothing there of interest and ducked beyond the vehicle and into the trees, heading now for the thudding noises which were still audible not far away. Closing stealthily on the sounds, Jardin avoided both the dead sticks underfoot and any foliage that might brush his garments noisily, coming suddenly upon a mossy rectangular hollow in which two men clad in dirty range garments were labouring, the taller with a doublejack and the shorter with a spade. Looking out upon the pair through a veil of leaves, Jardin saw that they were digging what could only be a grave, and this sent his eyes darting past them—to where, under the eastern wall of the grotto, a human form lay tightly shrouded in grey blankets.

What he was witnessing, then, were the preparations for a secret burial. As this was almost certainly Box H land, it appeared that somebody had died on the Harper ranch in a manner which the people involved would prefer the population in general—and no doubt the law in particular—not to know about. Murder at once sprang to mind as the more or less

131

inevitable reason for such a burial—and Jardin thought of the Texans who had been shot down in the gun battle with the herd-cutters a few hours ago—but there was still some uncertainty as to the number and fact of those deaths, and the matter did not seem to belong with the present burial. The single interment essayed here had a kind of 'separate' feeling about it, and his imagination flew unprompted to the shots which he had fired in the night at Sam Carter's killer. At least one of the slugs had hit the bushwhacker and, as his earlier reasoning had pointed to the killer's crime having been commissioned about here, it could be that the murderer had returned to his employer and died some time thereafter.

Yes, the notion was highly speculative —and had an element of supposition about it—but Jardin found himself with a strong desire to examine the corpse yonder and also with the glimmerings of an idea that could definitely link Sam Carter's death to the unexpected passage of Tom Tupper's herd through Blue Grass Valley and the horrifying incident in which the herd-cutters had been so bloodily involved. Yet, short of revealing himself—and using a gun to force the grave-diggers to back off—how was the examination of the body to be achieved and his deductions perhaps advanced to the point where they uncovered the truth behind the pattern of crime with which he was convinced he had made contact?

The sense of frustration was again almost unbearable in Jardin, but he checked his impulse to rashness. It seemed that only patience could do it. He would come back later, carrying a spade of his own, and disinter the corpse. Night must be the time for that. Vital things were seldom achieved conveniently, and he would just have to accept the need to go over his ground again at an hour and in circumstances that he would have preferred to avoid.

Just then, however, as he confirmed this latest plan with himself and was getting ready to turn and creep away from his edge of the shadowy grotto, the shorter of the two grave-diggers straightened up abruptly and threw his spade aside. 'Chesney, I've had enough o' this!' he declared. 'What we're doin' here for Dave Harper and that Roscoe fellow ain't good. I reckon that should give us some privileges. I'm votin' us a rest, my son. We'll take the cart to where them other bodies were hid, then load 'em up and bring 'em here.'

'Okay, Fred,' the taller man said doubtfully. 'The boss can't exactly quarrel with that—nor George Roscoe neither. Whatever we do, it has to be one thing at a time, and first as last sorta covers it, as you might say.'

'You've got it first time, Chesney,' Fred growled rebelliously. 'Tell you what, mister: go to hell if I'm going to dig individual graves along this hollow either! Them Texas boys are all goin' into the same hole. Why should we sweat our innards out doing it so nice?'

'Can't see that it matters much,' Chesney allowed. 'The thing's to get 'em buried up and this place made ship-shape. We've gotta try to wipe out all trace of these burials. If they get found, it'll be a hanging job for somebody.'

'Won't it just!' the shorter man gritted. 'With you and me somewhere in the line.'

'We ain't killed nobody!' Chesney yelped.

'Tell that to the judge, my son!' Fred spat, moving to the southern edge of the hollow and starting to climb over it. 'Well, are you comin'?'

'We can't leave Ace Pettit lyin' there like that!' Chesney protested.

'In the ground or otherwise, he ain't goin' to care!' Fred announced callously, out of the grotto now and shouldering away into the undergrowth beyond.

'Aw, blast it!' Chesney spluttered, looking first at the shrouded body and then scowling after his partner. 'Aw, dammit-to-helll' Then he went scrambling into the shorter man's wake, and strode off rapidly to catch up with him.

Jardin let his right knee settle firmly on the ground. Releasing a pent up breath, he listened in a fully relaxed state to the fading noises that traced the withdrawal of the grave-diggers from the wood. He wondered

135

how that evil, dirty pair would feel could they know how closely they had just been overlooked and how damning their talk had sounded to his ear. They would undoubtedly regard his spying as reason for murder, and that brought home to him fully for the first time the seriousness of what he had become engaged in. If he got caught around here now, it would surely be the death of him. For he had already seen and learned too much. It appeared to him that the men on the other side were now attempting an almost impossible cover-up, and the desperation of such men had never known any bounds. If, then, they were that desperate, he must exercise an equal care. But how could anybody do what had to be done here without taking foolhardy risks?

Rising, Jardin stepped away from his cover and jumped down into the grotto. He walked at once to the shrouded form lying at the end of the hollow on his left. After studying the tightly wrapped body for a few moments, he perceived that the binding blanket had been secured in place by the use of three outsize safety pins. He unfastened these; then, grabbing the end of the cloth which had been freed, pulled on it hard, spinning the body out of its shroud and then watching it settle to rest on its back.

The dead man, clothed in black shirt and trousers, presented a stiff, pale-faced figure, and it appeared probable that he had given up the ghost a day ago. In life, he could have been no ornament to the human race, for he had a thin, sour, ratlike face, narrow shoulders, slightly buckled hips and spindly limbs. The tall Chesney had called him Ace Pettit, and Jardin could remember having heard of a hired gun with that name—so the deceased's role in the world seemed to have fitted in with Jardin's earlier thoughts concerning Sam Carter's murder. Now, turning the body over—since he could discern no wound on the front of it—Jardin saw a bullet-hole fairly high on the right-hand side of the dead man's torso. Well, the hit had been in the right spot to have been fired at a fleeing horseman's back by a man seated on the ground, so this pointer, too, fitted his theory. Nor did the apparent time element quarrel with it either; for, as he recalled from dealing with the company wounded during the war, a man hit high in the liver could live on quite actively for some while before succumbing. This man could indeed have been Big Sam's killer.

Feeling that it would be singularly ill-advised to waste time here on prolonged reflections, Jardin wrapped the corpse up again—using plenty of strength in the process—and then replaced the three extra large safety pins at the end of the blanket in the same securing positions as they had occupied before, thus leaving the grim package with its original appearance. After that he lifted the shrouded body back to its former resting place and climbed quickly out of the grotto again—knowing that he had reason to be satisfied with himself, yet feeling nothing of the sort.

Acutely watchful still, and moving with extreme caution, Jardin started returning to where he had left his horse, his brain again working flat out, for he could see a weakness in his latest reasoning that had always been apparent but now assumed its full importance. If the murder of Sam Carter had, as he suspected, been carried out in his trail camp to ensure the revival and persistence of the old feud between the Carters and the Jardins—in order to give Dave Harper and George Roscoe, in their capacities of landowner and herd-cutter, the excuse to advise the oncoming herds from Texas that it was no longer safe to pass through Buffalo Valley, because the farmers who lived there had resumed shooting at each other—then it would have been necessary for somebody in the Carter household to have said in Dave Harper's hearing that Sam intended riding out to meet him, Jardin, on his way home from the Crippled Indian Mine. But if, as Sam Carter and his sister Rosemary had said, only they had known of Sam's plan to meet Jardin and end the feud, then only one or the other of them could have spoken so foolishly. It was unbelievable that Sam could have done anything of the sort, and the same that Rosemary could have done such a thing; so, strong as he felt his case against Harper and Roscoe to be, the particular snag which he had just examined appeared to leave him with a lot of circumstantial evidence but no causal linkage; for the boss of the Box H would simply have had to know about Big Sam's mission up the trail before the bushwhacker could have been despatched and the rest of the plot evolved—which had obviously included the invitation for the trail-herders to use the Blue Grass Valley instead of their usual route across this part of Kansas. All mention of the proposed herd-cutting would, of course, have been avoided, since it appeared obvious that this thinning out was the motive for it all. It had to be that the cows extracted from Tupper's and subsequent herds were intended for re-branding and inclusion among the beeves on the Box H, probably with a fifty/fifty division of profits between Dave Harper and George Roscoe once the marketing had been done.

Reaching the edge of the wood, Jardin

first made sure that the grave-diggers had indeed left with their cart and passed from sight, then went to the bush behind which he had tethered his horse and freed the brute, climbing back into his saddle and looking through the wood as he had before. Seeing no reason to alter the line of travel which he had previously fixed on, Jardin set off into the timber and spent the next few minutes ducking branches and rounding clumps of undergrowth. But progress was easy enough, and he reached the eastern side of the wood without any problem or check.

Emerging from the trees, he entered a spread of grazing land which fanned about ten degrees on his left hand and far more widely on his right. The ranch buildings of the Box H were visible down the wider angle as a display of grey tiles, reddish timbers, metal pens and a windpump. On Jardin's reckoning, the body of Blue Grass Valley began to open over that way; and, if he rode straight on, using what cover the land offered, he should soon cross the ground which Tupper's herd had earlier traversed and then cut the trail to Standish a few miles further on. He need have no reluctance to visit the sheriff's office now, for he had seen more than enough on this ranch to justify action by the law; and he would even be prepared to make a statement as to how Sam Carter had died—and for what reason, as he had deduced it. Pull in Harper, Roscoe, and the other villains, and somebody in that dishonourable company would soon start spilling his guts; and Jardin had no doubt that most of his theories concerning the crime hereabouts would soon be confirmed.

All seemed tranquil around Jardin and his cantering mount. The hush of the morning was profound, and the land was starting to warm to the yellow glow of the climbing sun. He could smell the sap in the prairie grass and the dryness of the earth under what little moisture the dark hours had managed to protect from evaporation. A butterfly rocked past his head, and others fluttered up about his mount's hooves. The feeling of summer was strong upon the immediate scene and the far blue distance alike. Jardin put no more pressure on his clearly tired horse than he had to. Everything seemed to be going nicely. He had indeed mastered his problems for the moment.

Yet the very thought seemed to be enough. As if by some malign magic, another of those shouts of discovery went up. Once more Jardin's nerves jumped and his stomach turned over. Screwing his head round sharply to the left, he gazed across his shoulder and saw there—newly risen from folding earth and not more than a hundred yards away—those same four horsemen who had chased him so relentlessly an hour or so back.

But this was far more immediately serious than that earlier hunt had been, for the land was much flatter and its features offered no scope for manoeuvre. If the ageing horse under him had been more up to things, he might have outrun the four men yonder on a headlong dash eastwards, but his mount was already three-parts worn-out and would stand little chance when the enemy began their inevitable containing movements and forced the frequent changes of course that would do more to confuse and finally exhaust the old gelding than anything else.

Jardin was the desperate one now. It would be fruitless to start running again. Those fellows over there were already drawing their guns. There need be no restrictions on their shooting here. They were already in range, and it might be no more than a matter of seconds before one of them put a bullet in his back. His situation was damned near impossible, and he could only meet it head on. He must match fire with fire. True, they were four against one, but he had always been a good shot from the saddle and was confident of being able to give them plenty to think about.

Fetching up, he climbed his horse round, then jerked his revolver. He didn't see how this could work—but there was nothing else to try!

SEVEN

Thumbing back the hammer of his Colt, Jardin sent his mount charging at the oncoming horsemen. This tactic in itself was enough to upset his enemies—ranchmen, he was reasonably certain, though this had never been actually confirmed by word or event—from the Box H, and their first shots missed him by wide margins. His own first bullet, on the other hand, at least winged the man coming at him from farthest to the right, and the fellow lifted in his stirrups and cried out in pain before settling again.

The guns boomed and roared, blast and counter-blast, and the peace of the morning was but a memory now. Slugs laced the air, and powdersmoke hung in clouds about the windless scene. Twice Jardin felt his clothing touched by lead. He shrank small against these attempts to kill him, and his eyes were as merciless as those opposite as he followed his jinking targets with the muzzle of his 'Peacemaker' and squeezed off each time his sights met. He chipped a second man, then hit a third full in the body, but now his gun clicked emptily and he perceived that, though he had done much better than his enemies, he had not reduced the odds against him that significantly. With no hope of making a reload, he shoved his Colt away, then whirled his horse again and rode off rather aimlessly, perhaps seeking the aid of a miracle.

There was no miracle, however, and it suddenly occurred to Jardin that he was actually riding towards Dave Harper's ranch. Realizing that he could hardly do a more stupid thing than that, he tried to swing left—aiming again for the course that he had originally intended—but he discovered almost immediately that what he had feared at the initial contact was now happening, for one of the following riders had swung out to a position from which he could easily cut the angle involved and either meet Jardin sideways on or force him back into straight flight. Experimenting, he attempted a similar manoeuvre on the right, but found that the same counter measure was in operation there. He saw that he was being shepherded towards those not so distant ranch buildings by four men who, if a little shot about in three cases, were still very determined, and he realized there wasn't a lot he could do about it.

Jardin's nape and backbone crept. Like him, his followers had emptied their guns; but, unlike him, it was unnecessary for all four to give the whole of their attention to riding, and he feared it couldn't be long before one of the more dexterous present managed a reload in the saddle and began letting fly at his vulnerable back. Sighing heavily into his collar, Jardin had to admit the truth to himself. His latest efforts had hardly improved his position at all, and it still looked as if a bullet through the spine could be the end of him.

Then something totally unexpected occurred. His horse, seeming to pick up the despairing need in its rider's mind, suddenly defied the years and began to draw on reserves of stamina that few could have believed it possessed. It first speeded into great loping paces, then tucked tighter and fairly raced ahead. After half a mile or so, it had so outdistanced the mounts in its wake that Jardin found himself again contemplating a left turn and now with every chance of drawing clear of the semi-arc in which the pursuer on that side had been so easily able to out-manoeuvre him while the chase had been a close one. There was, of course, a big worry present. It was the question of how long his horse could keep up this remarkable effort before cracking; but obviously he could only do his best with what fate had sent and pray over the rest; so he began turning his mount eastwards in a manner that was unlikely to offend it and was soon running parallel with the now nearby ranch site and no longer towards it.

Jardin threw a glance back. His pursuers had no answer to what was happening. They, too, were forking over-used animals and falling back by a yard in every two. Jardin began to believe that he was going to achieve what had seemed impossible not long ago and make good his escape; but then, as he had seen happen so many times in his life, the unexpected produced more of the same. A rifle barked on his right, and he felt his mount shudder and break its stride. Then it flopped out, skidding a little on its belly, and Jardin was catapulted out of his saddle by the impact and flew over the shot creature's head, somersaulting. He struck the ground in full flow and went on rolling for about ten yards before coming to rest in a spreadeagled position and gazing into a sky that seemed to spin darkly despite the brightness of the hour. Seeking to rise, with the impulse to flight still strong in him, he found that he had no control over his limbs and had to desist. This, then, must be the finish. His worst fears had been fulfilled. He had fallen into the clutches of men who were bound to kill him.

Closing his eyes, Jardin fought his daze with all the powers of his mind and body.

Soon his brain ceased revolving quite so fast and he felt control over his person returning. Then he sensed people standing by and staring down at him. Opening his eyes again, he looked up and back at them. He made out his hunters sitting their mounts in the background—one man hunched over and appearing very poorly indeed—but closer to him stood a large, square-shouldered man, with a mallet-shaped jaw, Roman nose, weathered brow, and walrus moustache. He held a Winchester rifle in his hands—presumably the gun which had dropped the horse—and was now pointing it at Jardin's chest. Beside the big man stood the slightly taller George Roscoe, who wore the cruellest smile which the fallen man had ever seen on a human face. 'Hi, Jardin,' Roscoe greeted sardonically.

'Go to hell!' Jardin returned thickly.

'Nice to have friends, eh, Harper?' Roscoe inquired of his large companion. 'Tut, tut, Ben!'

'Twice!' Jardin snarled.

'Can't keep burning, boy!' Roscoe leered,

understanding him perfectly. 'Anyhow, I reckon you'll get to the hot place ahead of me!'

'What have you been doing on my land, Jardin?' Harper asked.

'Taking the morning air,' Jardin informed the rancher.

'And I'm the Queen of Sheba!' the rancher returned, utterly disbelieving.

'You've put your nose in where it ain't wanted!' Roscoe announced flatly. 'Bad habit of yours, Ben, and there's always a price to pay!'

'Forget about my nose!' Jardin rasped. 'You men dealt these cards.'

'What do you know?' Harper now asked quietly.

'How much does he know, Dave?' Roscoe corrected. 'Is it important? However much or little, it's got to be a sight too much for us!'

Hard and angry though Harper's features were, there was also a faint reluctance about the man, and he glanced round at the oldest of the four riders who had lately been chasing the prisoner about the

151

countryside—the only man of the quartet, indeed, who had not received some bullet-wound from Jardin—and said: 'I had to do your job for you just now, Parker.'

'That you did, boss,' the craggy Parker acknowledged. 'He was getting away again all right.'

'Well, it was clear to me he had to be stopped,' the rancher said dismissively. 'You told me just now you first spotted him shadowing that Texas herd.'

'Uh, huh.'

'He seemed to know what he was there for?'

Parker nodded. 'He sure galloped off fast enough when I bawled out. He's a tricky devil too. Made rare fools of me and these characters. Doubled back on us under the ridge west of here, and must have swung this way through yonder wood. Though he sure did take some time about it 'cos we were the better part of an hour forward of the time we lost him when we ran across him again just north of here.'

'He'd stopped someplace, Dave,' Roscoe observed quickly. 'It figures he saw something he shouldn't have in that wood—and stopped to do some snooping.' Working up spittle, he expelled it through his teeth. 'That's your man all right! I know him from of old!'

'Just like you know me, eh?' Harper commented a touch bitterly.

Roscoe shrugged, one corner of his mouth hiked in an insolent grin. 'We've done business before,' he agreed.

'To my cost,' Harper ground out, seemingly unable to check his tongue in the force of his barely controlled emotions. 'To my cost.'

'No—his,' Roscoe once more amended, though this time grittily. 'You mustn't get worried, Dave. We only seem to be in a mess. We're coming out of this okay. Straight faces, and plenty of bluff. As for Jardin, he's just another body to be delivered to those two boys of yours.'

'Don't bank on those two overmuch,' Harper warned. 'Fred Grout and Chesney Taylor aren't worth a lot. The strain on their loyalty is already more than I like.'

'Yeah,' Roscoe conceded knowingly,

'I've had a share of boys like that, Dave. Well, you've hired a real hard man in your foreman there—Don Parker—and all you need do is have him take that pair aside and give them what they need to be going on with. It never fails!'

'It may work with the dog, the woman, and the walnut tree,' Harper mused grimly, 'but you can never tell with men.'

'It's a sure moral you can only trust a dead one,' Roscoe remarked, sounding openly impatient with the cattleman now. 'If you haven't got the guts or brains for this, Dave, you'd better let me handle it from now on.'

'You can't murder him here!' Harper protested, his expression a warning one. 'You and those bungling idiots of yours have done enough of that already!'

'What a shame!' Roscoe mocked, while pretending to soothe. 'All for that little extra, eh? What greed can do for a man! You were just as edgy years ago when you were buying up rustled stock. Nice business you've got here, Dave. It'd be a crying shame if you lost it all!'

'That's enough, George!' Harper almost choked. 'Blood has been spilled today!'

'That's new?' Roscoe queried. 'Sam Carter's wasn't enough? His murder was your doing first and foremost, my man. You can only hang once, and you made a provisional booking with George Maledon when you hired Ace Pettit and his rifle.'

'You keep the hangman's name out of this!' Harper breathed, the tough, lived-in patina of his face seeming to hover now upon the ashen pallor which suddenly underlay it. 'Nothing can alter the mess you and those thieves of yours made across the way!'

'We can ride off if you want,' Roscoe yawned.

'That'd be about your mark, wouldn't it?' the cattleman snarled.

'Damned if it would!' Roscoe retorted. 'Oh, sure, I'd ride off and leave you to stew in it most any time, but I've money tied up here. We'll break up that Texas herd later on, drive the bits off to various places we know, and brand 'em up anew. We can sell 'em the same up in Abilene.

155

There's market enough in Chicago for the buyers not to be interested in new burns. It's no trick bamboozling the law these days. Sheriffs are honest men, and they've got to do their jobs honestly. It surely puts them at a disadvantage.'

'You make me sick, Roscoe!' the rancher declared.

'So you can puke in each of those hiding places you've got around,' Roscoe informed him. 'Keep your nerve, like I say, and we'll come through! If you haven't got what it takes to blow Jardin's brains out, let me take him into your barn and do it.'

'Very well,' Harper said, snapping to keep the note of defeat low in his voice. 'This is more your game than mine, George. Those who sup with the devil should use a long spoon.'

'I'm not rightly sure I understand that one, Dave,' Roscoe said, signalling for Jardin to get off the ground. 'You've got a heap more education than I have. But it sounds to me like you broke a good rule somewhere.'

Jardin clambered slowly erect. He watched

156

the rancher's jaw sinking towards the stud that held together the collar of his raw-necked shirt. Amidst all else, he felt a trace of contemptuous pity for Dave Harper, whom he saw as trapped in a hopeless situation that the infamous Roscoe meant to exploit in every way that he could. 'Why don't you run?' Jardin asked insidiously. 'It might be the very thing for that snooty wife and daughter of yours if you went and left them. It's your only chance, Harper. Maledon will get you if you don't.'

'Shut up!' the rancher warned, his finger tightening on the trigger of his Winchester as the rifle's muzzle jerked into line with the prisoner's heart. 'This is no place for you to be giving advice!'

Jardin shrugged. He supposed the cattleman was right at that. He ought to be doing all in his power to encourage Harper to stay where the law could get at him. He had spoken oddly out of turn. Yet folk said and did things that were mildly irrational at times, and he imagined that the words he had just uttered were no more than his deeper intelligence trying to drive a wedge between his enemies by sounding vaguely sympathetic towards the rancher and considerate on his behalf. If Harper should try to escape his fears by heading for the hills—but reason told Jardin that was no more likely than the chance that he would still be alive at noon today. There was always the reality that a man had to face—the one that his imagination shied away from but his mind couldn't beat.

Harper spoke a gruff word. The riders present drew their horses round and headed towards the bunkhouse. After receiving a prod in the back from the rancher, Jardin moved shakily into the horsemen's tracks, making for the heart of the home site, where the house and barn stood on opposite sides of a yard that was shaded by tall elm trees. Still a little muddled in his thinking, it came to Jardin that he had no memory of anybody removing the empty revolver from his holster. If the weapon were still at his waist, he had wild visions of doing heroic things with it; but, on looking down, he saw that his enemies had made no mistake and the weapon had not been left with him. It occurred to him that it had most probably jumped leather when he had whirled through that series of somersaults after his horse had collapsed with Harper's bullet in it. Throwing back his head, he breathed deeply, gathering his wits and his courage. It was no good clutching at straws; this remained about as bad as it could be. Every step was taking him closer to what he imagined would be that darksome corner where a bullet fired by George Roscoe would either puncture his heart or scatter his brains, bringing instant oblivion.

Coming to the ranch house, they walked along its northern wall and passed into the yard at the rear of the dwelling. The barn now stood less than fifty paces away. Jardin deviated slightly, then felt steering pressure from the barrel of Harper's rifle, first on the top of the his left arm and then the right. He responded accordingly, because he could do nothing else. The great door at the front of the building yonder stood open. It seemed to yawn at him, and the gloom beyond the dusty threshold appeared to reach back into that crepe-spun eternity where there would be no single echo of the Ben Jardin story left. It was a weird notion, and Jardin shrank from it as he would have done a poison chalice.

'Getting scared, Ben?' Roscoe taunted. 'It's a far cry from Chancellorsville and Gettysburg, eh? Those places you had a cartridge in the barrel and the spike at the muzzle of your Springfield. Sure, it was butcher's work—but you had a chance. There's none here!'

'Many a slip, George,' Jardin reminded, trying to sound jaunty.

'Yeah,' Roscoe allowed, his wicked chuckle expressing total doubt.

Suddenly a woman's voice called to them from the back door of the house. This shout was the prelude to a couple of surprises for Jardin. The first was that the woman on the step—standing with a cobweb brush in her right hand and a housemaid's turban on her soft brown hair—was Adah Carter, wife of Frank, and clearly over from Buffalo Valley to do the cleaning work here, while the second was that the man who now appeared from the kitchen behind her was the tough little Abe Holst, sheriff of Standish. At the moment Adah partially obscured the lawman, but he put her aside with a nod of thanks and gestured for her to re-enter the house. This she did immediately, closing the door behind her.

'Sheriff,' Harper greeted rather tautly. 'What do you want?'

'To speak with you, Mr Harper,' the lawman answered.

'You can see where I am.'

Brown-shirt and britched, Holst left the back step and began advancing across the yard towards the three men who now stood waiting for him. His face wore a stern expression and he was already watching the trio opposite him with a questioning eye.

'You hold your row, Ben!' Roscoe hissed in Jardin's ear. 'Force me, boy, and I'll blast you anyhow!'

'Asking for it, wouldn't you say?' Jardin scorned in his turn. 'This looks like it for you, George!'

'He's one man, Ben,' Roscoe grated— 'and we don't know what he wants yet.'

'Sing small,' Harper warned, an apprehensive tremor in his voice—'both of you.'

Then the sheriff was with them. He halted a couple of paces away and, considering them with chin dipped and eyes wide open, tucked his thumbs behind the buckle of his gunbelt and said, 'What's happened to the Tupper herd, Mr Harper?'

'Happened?' Harper queried. 'How the deuce would I know, Holst? I imagine it's making its way a few miles north of here by now.'

'You're sure?'

'How can I be certain of a thing like that?' the rancher asked reasonably enough. 'I let Tupper's herd pass through my Blue Grass Valley, and that's where my concern ended.'

'Why did you let them through here, Mr Harper?'

'Because Tupper requested it.'

'Would that be normal?'

'You know it wouldn't, Sheriff.'

'Why, then?'

'Tupper and his men had heard rumours of a new outbreak of feuding in Buffalo Valley.'

Holst gave a slow and judicious nod, looking at Jardin now. 'I understand Sam Carter is dead, and I've been told you brought his body home.'

'That's right, Sheriff,' Jardin said. 'It would have been Adah Carter who told you.'

The lawman nodded his head again. 'What are you doing over this way, Ben?'

Jardin felt the cautionary touch of Roscoe's boot against his own, and he saw the other's hand lift fractionally towards his holster. 'Oh, I've been riding around.'

'He's looking for work,' Harper said.

'What's that rifle all about?' Holst demanded. 'I had the impression you were threatening him with it just now.'

'What an idea!' the rancher scoffed dismissively. 'His horse fell out there on the grass. It had to be destroyed. I used this rifle to shoot it.' He lowered his Winchester into the trail position. 'You can

163

go and see for yourself if you like. Jardin lost his own gun at the time he fell.'

'Happens,' the sheriff conceded, but it was uncertain as to just how much he believed.

'You've heard all about us,' Harper said. 'I suppose I have the right to ask what you're doing over here?'

'Yes,' Holst said, 'you have that right. I'm here because I had a visitor an hour or two ago. Jardin's sister Emma. She gave me to understand her brother Ben was out courting trouble to the north of Blue Grass Valley—where a cutting of the Tupper herd had gone wrong. She added, Ben, that you'd told her you thought the biggest crime you'd ever dreamed had been committed around here. It might even join up with the killing of Sam Carter—which did happen way out of my jurisdiction, else you'd be for it.'

'Harsh words, Sheriff!' Harper observed. 'I can't answer for Ben Jardin and his pipe dreams, but it's been quiet enough around here. Don't you find it so yourself?'

'Seems all right,' Sheriff Holst admitted.

'Smoke opium, do you, Jardin?'

'Damned if I do!'

'Then you don't have pipe dreams,' the lawman commented. 'You're no big drinker either, as I recall.'

'The odd beer.'

'That's what I mean. You've got the reputation for being a good worker and a responsible man.'

'It's not up to me to pass any comment on that, Sheriff,' Jardin said.

'People speak well of you all round, Ben.'

'You trying to piddle up his back, Sheriff?' Roscoe asked, adding a laugh that was openly disdainful.

'No,' the lawman said easily. 'I reckon I was trying to hint that I'm better disposed to believe him than I am some others.'

'Meaning us, I suppose?' Roscoe said, nodding at Harper while poking a thumb into his own midriff.

'You were reported in town yesterday.'

'What about it?'

'Your name's Roscoe, isn't it?' the sheriff queried.

'I've made no secret of it.'

'There's a Roscoe wanted all over the Southwest.'

'This ain't the Southwest,' Roscoe reminded. 'I've got two or three brothers—depending on what the war left—and there are other families of the Roscoe name.'

'All maybe true,' the lawman said. 'But you don't have the face of a good man.'

'What sort of face does a good man have, Sheriff?' Roscoe inquired. 'One like yours?'

Holst met the mocking Roscoe eye to eye, but said nothing.

'Like him, perhaps?' Roscoe suggested, indicating Dave Harper.

Again the lawman said nothing.

At that Harper took umbrage. 'Look to your job, Holst!' he warned. 'I not only have a face, Sheriff, but I have a big say in the community.'

'That's because you have a lot of money,' Holst said.

'I have a lot of money because I have a lot of cattle.'

'But did you get them all honestly?' the

166

lawman wondered thoughtfully. 'I've heard rumours.'

'Oh—oh, you have, have you?' Harper spluttered. 'Are you hinting I keep rustled stock on my range?' He made a grand, sweeping gesture. 'I give you permission to search where you like.'

'I could get it anyhow,' the sheriff reminded grimly. 'Your land will be searched all right, never fear. First, though, I'm taking the three of you back into town with me, and I aim to lock you, Mr Harper, and Roscoe there, into the strongest cell I've got. I'm not sure about Ben Jardin. I'll most likely take him riding with me. I'll be surprised if he hasn't got things to show me.'

'You can't do this, Holst!' Harper protested. 'You absolutely can't!'

'You haven't a blind thing to hold us on!' Roscoe added.

'You're wrong about that,' Holst said coldly. 'Did you figure I came here purely on a girl's say-so? I've been happy to let you talk, as I wanted to hear what you had to say. There's a young Texan lying wounded over at Jardin's farm in Buffalo Valley, and he's ready to spill his guts about a band of so-called official herd-cutters and the near massacre they carried out not long after sunup today.'

Roscoe listened to no more, and before Jardin—or even Harper—could do anything about it, he plucked out his Colt and shot Sheriff Holst through the heart.

EIGHT

Jardin stared down at the man who now lay dead and bleeding before him. The image shocked him through and through—and he wanted to yell at Heaven in his rage—yet he knew that he had no real loyalty here except to himself. Then he perceived that even the vile Roscoe was stunned by the brutal instantaneousness of what he had done—while Dave Harper stood in the grip of sheer horror—and Jardin realized that, for this particle of time, he was the last thing on his captors' minds. Trying to match physical action to the speed of his thoughts, he sent Harper staggering with a powerful push, then swung on Roscoe and thrust his right leg behind both the villain's lower limbs, cupping his right palm over the other's chin and literally throwing him to the ground.

Now, angling for the eastern wall of the barn, Jardin darted away from his sprawling victims. He was intent on pursuing the long way round to a horse—the late sheriff's, he suspected—which stood isolated at the opposite end of the ranch yard; since he judged that, if he attempted running to the brute over the shorter and open route, either Roscoe or Harper would recover before he got there and put a bullet in him. He hoped, however, that if he moved circuitously his enemies would miss his true intent and that he would be able to draw them into a chase in which he could baffle, confuse, and possibly deny them the clear shot at him that was so important.

Racing flat out, he reached the front corner of the barn that offered his first shelter. In the same moment he heard Roscoe bawl at Harper to get up and join him in giving chase. Ducking into what cover the timbers of the barn provided just there, he scampered down the eastern side of the big building and strained for its further end, the crack of a revolver shot sounding just before he got there and splinters whirling off the tree-sized cornerpost directly ahead of him. Two more bullets, cuffed rather than triggered, sought him in swift succession, both missing him by tiny margins, but then he was round the corner and out of immediate danger again, his eyes seeking further cover.

He saw bushes ahead of him, where the rear wall of the barn ended and the first of the great elms which bordered the western side of the ranch yard reared upwards and created a light-spangled mushroom of shade over the building's gable end. Calculating anew, he entered the bushes, forcing and ripping through them—a process that brought him a number of lacerations and was often extremely

170

painful—then, bursting clear where the dense growth ended, paused just the instant necessary to make sure that he was being directly pursued.

He heard booted feet trampling over the path that he had already marked—but a sudden thrill of uneasiness went through him nevertheless; for, though he could see no figure from here, he received the impression that only the lighter George Roscoe was actually chasing him in the direct sense. So, if that were the fact of it, what had become of Dave Harper? Had the rancher fallen too heavily to rise at once and join Roscoe in the pursuit? Or had he anticipated the escaper's possible ruse and run over to where the horse stood waiting? If he had done that, this piece of craft could end in nothing but futility.

Short of any additional inspiration, Jardin picked up to a run again and carried on as before. He threaded a swift course through the clumps of brush which now appeared in front of him; then, coming left, followed the green shrubs that grew behind the trunks of the leafy elms that darkened all the area, only angling towards the ranch yard again when he deemed that he was approaching its further end and should now emerge near the horse that he aimed to leap astride and ride to safety.

The undergrowth remained a bigger problem than he had expected. Holly and brambles suddenly formed a barrier in his path. There was no time to turn aside and seek an easier route, so he charged through the thorns and spiked foliage, the springy congestion of the growth across his body building to the extent that it almost stopped him in his tracks; but, as much by weight as power, he burst through the last of the impeding mass and staggered out into the yard, bits and pieces of dead briar and holly flaking off his garments as he made for the horse which to his relief he now saw was still standing by itself as before.

Reaching the mount, Jardin seized its trailing reins and speared the near side stirrup with his left toe, following the mount's sidling movement away from his sudden and unfamiliar presence. Stepping up, he filled the saddle with more accuracy than grace, and he would have galloped off without more ado; but just then a peremptory shout issued from the back door of the nearby house and he turned his gaze to see Dave Harper standing on the threshold with a pistol pressed to Adah Carter's head. The woman was kicking and screaming and doing everything in her power to break free from the cattleman's powerful left arm, but she didn't have a hope, and there was a look of utter pleading on her small and pretty features as the rancher yelled: 'What is it to be, Jardin?'

There was no choice. Harper appeared to be three-parts off his rocker. He would undoubtedly put a slug in Adah's brain if ignored. Jardin could not let it happen. He reined back on his horse, which was already bunched up to surge into flight, and sprang back to the ground just as Roscoe re-entered the ranch yard from amidst the nearer bushes and Harper began advancing from the rear door of the dwelling with his pistol still held as firmly as ever against the weeping but now less frantic Adah Carter's head.

'Well, I'll be jiggered!' Roscoe panted, summing up what had happened at a glance. 'If you ain't the prince of fools, Ben! You were clear and away!'

'That's right,' Jardin agreed shortly—far from sure that he had not indeed been a fool; for he had no doubt that his enemies still meant to kill him, and he could not see but that the unfortunate Adah, witness to so much, would have to die too. 'Beat you every time, don't I?'

'Crow, you two-bit sodbuster!' Roscoe spat. 'What's so special about the petticoat, Dave? She got some kind of claim on Ben Jardin?'

'Hell, no!' Harper responded. 'She's a member by marriage of the family the Jardins have been feuding with since Adam was a pup!'

'I don't get that!' Roscoe protested irritably.

'First,' Harper exclaimed, 'it isn't in the nature of Ben Jardin to let a woman die for him, and second, the feud's over and

I reckoned Jardin—if he did come for that horse—would want to let his behaviour prove it. But what's far more to the point, it was already obvious to me that we can't let Adah Carter leave here alive. She must realize now that it was her gossipy tongue that told me how she overheard Sam, her brother-in-law, and Rosemary, Sam's sister, discussing how he aimed to ride up the Garden City trail and meet Ben Jardin to end the feud between their families and then persuade him to join forces and make a little money out of the Texas trailherds passing through.'

'The idea from which you got your ideas,' Roscoe said, 'and all this mischief arose.'

'You'd been around asking for work,' Harper reminded. 'I did my best to oblige.'

'Am I denying it?' Roscoe asked querulously. 'You're a better thinker than you are doer, Dave—that's your trouble. Still, with that sheriff dead we may yet be able to get out of this without losing much we've gained along the way. Your lawman is just another body to bury with the rest. I'll visit

175

Buffalo Valley after that and finish off that g'damned Texan who managed to slink away from our shoot-out this morning. I'll wipe out the Jardin family too. All the gabby tongues around should be still when I've finished there. Then we'll need no more than enough time to break up the Tupper herd and clear the land yonder. No impossible job.'

'There'll be questions a-plenty asked about Sheriff Abe Holst in town,' Harper reminded.

'So what?' Roscoe demanded indifferently. 'Will that matter so long as nothing's found? I don't think so. Who's going to risk trespassing on the Box H? Ain't done, m'friend! You've got a reputation. Everybody knows Dave Harper keeps Don Parker and some real tough hombres on his payroll.'

'It might be done,' Harper admitted hesitantly. 'Perhaps we could bluff it through. Talk and guesswork don't add up to a lot at that. If the reason is there, I can cut up real mean, and nobody blames a man for getting riled when others accuse where they can't prove.'

'That's my man!' Roscoe applauded. 'We'll do what we've gotta do, then hold strong. Everything will work out for us, you'll see. It's all about nerve, Dave—nerve!'

'Yes, I can see you're right, George,' Harper agreed, brightening, and the upsurge of his courage seemed about to consolidate.

But just then the softly moaning Adah Carter rolled a pleading eye at him and said: 'You won't hurt me, will you, Mr Harper? You've always been a real good boss, sir. That's why I've been so ready to ride over here two or three times a week and do the housework. Let me go, sir—please.' She added what she appeared to think must be the clinching argument. 'I've got children at home!'

'Stop whining, woman!' Harper ordered sharply. 'I cannot abide a woman who blubbers and begs!'

'Let's walk them into the barn,' Roscoe said, a sadistic grin flaring evilly into the lines of the thin skin that covered his narrow-boned face. 'I'll do 'em in right away. Once they're dead, we'll be free to get on with our work.'

'Oh, you wicked men!' Adah Carter bleated breathlessly. 'You can't get away with it. Sheriff Holst told me you couldn't.'

Harper gave her a brief but hard shake, then demanded: 'What did that varmint tell you?'

'He told me,' the woman went on, somewhere between the lachrymose and the defiant, 'that he left written word for his deputy about this place before he left town. When he fails to get home, there'll be a posse riding out here, sure as fate!'

'My God!' Harper exclaimed, quite aghast. 'Like that, George, there's nothing we can keep quiet!'

'Don't talk so damned silly!' Roscoe flung back. 'Holst didn't really know anything. He was still surmising. He's dead, but the fact still stands ahead of that. Maybe that bitch is lying too! She could be cleverer than she looks! Anyhow, let the posse come. We can still bluff it out.

Didn't I say, Dave—nerve, that's what it's all about. And didn't you admit just now that you could see it for yourself?'

'It all begins to seem—too much.'

'Stick it!' Roscoe warned. 'Do you want to swing?'

'No—no!'

'Then stick it!'

The rancher took an enormous breath, his face purplish and screwed up as he held the air a few moments and subdued his panic. 'All right—all right.'

'Let's get over to the barn then!' Roscoe insisted, jiggling his revolver on and off cock. 'March!'

They began heading for the barn. Jardin walked down the yard with a firm tread, but Adah Carter started kicking and screaming again and forced Harper to drag her along. 'Will you shut up?' he seethed. 'I don't want my wife and daughter out here! I want to keep them out of this!'

'Ditto!' Roscoe snarled, screwing a half turn as he walked and delivering a short backhander that hit the woman in the face with force enough to shock her into silence and leave her dribbling blood. 'That's better.'

They reached the barn moments later, and had just passed into the structure's musty gloom through the main door, when two horsemen galloped into the ranch yard and angled towards the front of the big storage building, clattering to a halt near the threshold and peering indoors at the four figures who had just stepped inside. Craning, Jardin recognised the two newcomers as the leery, hare-lipped Jockey Dunn and the gap-toothed, razor-scarred Olly Bowes, two of the more prominent members of what he had lately come to think of as Roscoe's gang.

'What the heck do you boys want?' snapped the plainly annoyed gang-boss, who had also turned his head at the sound of the horses and now checked his company in the barn with an impatient sign.

'What are you biting at us for?' Olly Bowes inquired aggrievedly, his older person bearing the marks of one who had swallowed dust and run sweat for longer than he should have done. 'We're only obeyin' the orders you give us.'

'That's right, George,' Jockey Dunn affirmed, his Southern lilt at once manifesting. 'Yoh said me an' Olly could ride over to the ranch house an' git fed once them beeves was settled down and out o' sight. We was up watchin' them Texas boys and their herd through most o' the night. Seems to me yoh has forgot, my man.'

'Blast you, Jockey—no!' Roscoe lied. 'I'm a busy man right now. I've got me a couple of shootings to do.'

'Them two?'

'Of course them two!'

'Shuah makes yoh think, don't it?' Jockey drawled philosophically, though his writhing mouth matched the insidious leering of his opaque eyes. 'There was you and that Mr Jardin a-punchin' each other's haids yesterday mornin'. Now here yoh is goin' to shoot the feller. And that there pretty little woman too. It makes a man think, that it does.' He passed a hand under his steep, sharp nose, snuffling. 'What's she done, George?'

'Mostly turned up in the wrong place at the wrong time, I'd say,' Roscoe answered shortly. 'Sure, it's a waste and all that—in a land that's short of women—but needs must, eh?'

'Well, do we get fed or not?' Olly Bowes demanded.

'I fear it will have to be not,' Harper said. 'Sorry. Mrs Carter was to get the grub.'

'Hang that for a story!' Bowes snorted.

'Dave doesn't want to involve his women in any of this,' Roscoe explained. 'Better not too. They're not our kind.'

'Well, she ain't dead yet, is she?' Bowes asked, nodding at Adah Carter and making it plain that he yielded nothing to the needs of his belly. 'Lookee here, young Roscoe! You promised Jockey and me cooked grub and a rest if we did what you wanted. We done it. Now you keep your end!'

'I never heard anything like it!' Roscoe howled. 'There's you kicking up all this fuss about what I said hours ago. Do you realize how serious matters are, Olly?'

'No,' Bowes said implacably, 'and I don't care. I'm blamed hungry, and I got the gut-ache from it. I ain't et in a whole day. Nor's Jockey.'

'Well, you don't hear him complaining about it,' Roscoe pointed out. 'You guys have gone without grub for a week before now.'

'When we had to,' Bowes reminded.

'He's only asking you to keep your word, George,' Jockey Dunn said gently.

'Now you're at it too,' Roscoe said unpleasantly.

'No, suh,' Jockey contradicted. 'Just playin' honest Injun.'

'We can't go on like this, George!' Harper announced impatiently. 'Mrs Carter is still alive. We must make use of her. Adah, will you feed them?'

'Yes, sir,' the woman hastened, her mouth and eyes opening wide and her hands working feverishly. 'I'll feed them the best meal they've ever had!'

'I'm sure you will,' the rancher agreed dryly. 'Any reprieve is better than none.' He ran an eye over the male prisoner.

'What do you aim to do about Jardin, George? Carry on as planned?'

'I figure I'll save him,' Roscoe drawled vindictively. 'Never did meet a guy who liked to do his killing by halves. I'll finish 'em off together. Reckon I need some chow too. It could be a while before we get the chance to feed again. Jockey—Olly! Get your butts down here! I want you to find a dark corner—way back from the door—and tie Jardin up.' His eyes became like agates. 'You do a good job of it now—or I'll skin you both alive!'

'We'll make as good a job of it as you would,' Olly Bowes responded scornfully.

'See that you do!' Roscoe advised portentously, spinning his Colt back into leather as Bowes and Dunn dismounted and the latter man drew his own revolver and covered Jardin.

'Get your ass off, George!' Bowes urged. 'We'll join you in the kitchen as soon as we've finished here.'

Nodding, Roscoe moved out of the barn and then stalked towards the house, while Harper and Mrs Carter pursued him at the distance of a few yards, the rancher now holding the woman by her left arm but leaving her more or less free to act as she liked. Now Olly Bowes lifted the lariat from his saddle and shook out the noose. 'Let's git on with it, Jockey,' he said. 'Betcha George inspects our knots before he salivates Jardin. We can't do much o' anything right for him these days.'

'We can't,' Dunn agreed, 'an' that's a fact. He's the worst guy I was ever bossed by!'

'You can always put a bullet in him,' Jardin observed.

'Hey, you!' Jockey rasped. 'Hold your g'damn Yankee noise!' Then he haw-hawed. 'Want to see George killed, huh? I figured you'd done it yourself yesterday.'

'There's no call to be friendly with him,' Bowes said.

'I wasn't bein' so!' Jockey Dunn protested, promptly knocking Jardin down with a short but well-timed right uppercut. 'There. Satisfied? Is it a sin to talk now?'

Jardin had gone straight down onto

his backside. He sat there looking up at the man who'd hit him. 'Thanks,' he muttered, using the index finger and thumb of his right hand to work tenderly at his chin. 'Thanks a lot.'

He made to rise, but was instantly pushed back onto his buttocks by Olly Bowes, who dropped the noose of his lasso over the prisoner's head and shoulders and yanked it tight. Bowes's expression was quite inconsequential as he trussed Jardin up in a truly professional manner and finished off with a series of knots so complicated that it would probably have been applauded on the deck of a whaler. 'That's you done up for all Eternity!' he yawned. 'That rope's never comin' off. We'll bury you in it!'

'Sort of gift to the devil,' Jockey Dunn spat.

'Aw, stop trying to be clever!' Bowes advised. 'It don't suit you, Jockey. just grab a-hold on the rope and let's drag him out of sight. All I want to do right now is eat, and the sight of that messed up face of his spoils my appetite!'

Dunn offered a single word of comment, but that got lost in a grunt as he seized a turn of Jardin's bindings and put out towing strength, his effort just less than enough to overcome the bound man's weight until Bowes added his power to the initial heave. After that the pair hauled Jardin across the barn, his canvas seat rasping on the brown mortar of the floor, and dumped him towards the rear of the building and near its left-hand wall, where the residual straw from an old pile formed a thick carpet on one side of him and a large mound of chopped logs loomed on the other.

Then, dusting off their hands, more for effect than from any need, the two villains walked away from Jardin—promising to 'be back soon'—and he watched them go, their shapes receding into the greater light of the building towards the door. They moved like very tired men, and no doubt needed a long spell of sleep, but he didn't doubt that they and their brutal leader would be back within the hour, and that he would be a fool to rely on having even that much time left to him.

Jardin's situation seemed hopeless, but he was much too afraid to give up just like that. He must at least try to get out of the mess that he was in, and he marshalled his forces, both mental and physical, accordingly. The shadows were thick back here, and he couldn't see much in detail, but his eyes quickly got used to the reduced light and he began to peer around him, looking for a snag or some kind of sharp edge on which to damage or—more hopefully—sever a round of his bindings, but there seemed absolutely nothing in sight to aid him in the slightest.

Discovering that he could roll around on the floor—providing he put out all his strength and was prepared to accept some painful knocks in the process—Jardin tumbled away from the spot on which he had been dumped, his imagination exercised by the presence of the piled firewood and the possibility that the tool which had been used to chop it could still be somewhere about. But his bruising peregrinations around the floor still revealed nothing to him by which he might free himself from his bonds and, after circling a chaff-cutter and the turnip-slicer next to it, not to mention dozens of piled sacks of grain, a cluster of fencing tools and materials, and much else, he returned to his starting point—breathless, sweaty, and aching—and rolled onto the straw, tipping onto his right side then and taking what comfort he could from the harsh and dusty carpet of wheat stems.

Shutting his eyes tightly, he fought for control of himself. It seemed that he had gone to the limit, and that there was no place else to go. He was going to be slaughtered very shortly like a pig in the shambles. He fought his bonds, writhing and twisting, but his panic would not abate, and all he did was hurt himself more than he had already been hurt. Then exhaustion hit him, and he was forced to give up the battle. His terror receded, and he felt the onset of resignation. What must be, must be, here as ever. Every man had to die in the end. It seemed that he must go sooner rather than later. Forget it—accept it; die like a man. There was nothing else. Had he not realized from the first what getting caught would mean?

Then he opened his eyes again and glanced up at the wall before him. As if his torment had been creative in itself, he saw, stark and simple in outline, what he had prayed to see several minutes ago: the axe with which the logs had been cut. The tool had been slipped into a kind of rack which had been formed by nailing a strip of timber fairly low down between two of the walls oaken uprights, and the end of the handle rested on the ground. Judging that he had been left enough freedom of movement in his lower legs, Jardin felt confident that he would be able to get in close enough to the haft to grip it between his feet and lift it upwards until the weight of its steel bit either toppled it out of the rack or left it so tilted away from the wall that he could kick it clear with a quick jerk of his toe.

It was as if he contemplated the answer to

every human ill. The fatigue fell away from him, and his fatalism likewise vanished. Turning his legs to the wall, he put his feet to work as he had visualised, and the axe lifted out of its slot and fell to the floor in a single smooth movement. It was done; and it could hardly have been more easy.

But then, inevitably, Jardin was confronted by the question of what exactly he had done. He had achieved nothing that left him any better off as yet. The axe was plainly a first class tool, and appeared to have a good edge on it; but he had yet to make the best use of that edge. It was difficult to see how he was to position the axe in order to bring his bindings and the blade together. He couldn't seem to come to terms with it, and time was dribbling away.

In an effort to clear his mind, he swallowed hard and gave his head a shake. A thousand mistakes were possible, and one or more of his captors could reappear at any moment and put an end to this latest escape attempt before it had really got started.

He simply must stop trembling and just act. So he acted—picking the axe up between his heels and placing it in the angle between the nearest upright post and the wall, with its bit inverted—but he didn't stop trembling. His brow hot and the tightness of his breathing almost unbearable, he shuffled round on his backside and forced himself towards the axe, using a thrusting movement of his heels, and he reached the slight upward tilt of the propped cutting edge without much difficulty and raised himself sufficiently to jam the axe handle into its resting place with the middle of his back and then start rubbing a lower turn of his bonds against the cutting edge.

The pressure he managed to apply was obviously too little for the quick results he sought, but he felt the well-honed steel begin to bite straightaway. Having got the process started, he knew that he mustn't let up—for he might not be able to exactly line up his initial cut with the axe blade again if he once let the rope slip out of position—and he shut his eyes and endured as seldom before, the sheer cramp and discomfort caused by his unbalanced crouch bringing still more sweat from his pores and the odd grunt of suffering from his lips.

He held on, and kept going. Suddenly the turn of the rope on which he had been working parted with a tiny jerk. But it made no difference, since Olly Bowes's final knotting had obviously been more widespread than the prisoner had supposed and secured all the concluding stages of the binding at different points. This forced Jardin to start all over again—his awareness of passing time a pressure that almost screwed the brain out of his head—and, cutting more by guesswork than anything else, he severed a second round of his bindings. This helped no more than the first, and only his feverish terror kept him going through what amounted to the torments of the damned before a third severance caused the lariat to burst apart at his heels and then fall loose all the way up his legs.

But even that was not enough to free

him—though it did allow him to stand up and work his arms against the turns of the rope which still held his upper body in thrall—and a further minute or two passed before he was able to first loosen his remaining bonds enough to shrink small thereafter and finally cast them off with a wriggle and heave.

He had done it. The rope now lay as a frayed and untidy presence at the foot of the pile of logs before him. But he felt more light-headed than triumphant and a hand seemed to reach down and strangle his guts as he heard voices out in the ranch yard and then what was obviously a yell of fury from George Roscoe. 'The skunk!' the gang-boss bellowed. 'I knew it—I knew it when he slunk out! That g'damned coward has run away! Dave Harper has taken that sheriff's horse and skedaddled! I'm going after him—and I'm going to catch him—I'm going to kill him!'

Jardin heard feet running towards the barn door. Picking up the axe with which he had freed himself, he stood ready.

NINE

The footfalls ceased their ominous approach a few yards short of the barn's threshold, and Jardin catfooted into a watcher's position at the front corner of the piled firewood. Looking out into the yard, he saw George Roscoe halted with Jockey Dunn and Olly Bowes. The three men were peering westwards—though what they could see in that direction for the great clns was difficult to say—and Jardin could only imagine that they regarded it as the probable way that Dave Harper had fled. Just then Roscoe turned to his companions and snarled: 'I'll have to leave it to you men to kill Ben Jardin and the Carter woman. Don't pull faces like that! There's nothing much to it! After you've done it, get the bodies over to the wood. Sheriff Holst's must go with them. I told you the story of how I came to shoot him.'

He used the heel of his right hand to jam down hard on the butt of his sixgun. 'Hell-and-dammit! Why can't things go right? This is getting to be a mess, boys!'

'What was that you said about that Texas feller lying over in Buffalo Valley?' Olly Bowes inquired. 'Didn't you say he'd got to be done in as well?'

'That's what I said!' Roscoe replied, at his most downright. 'That's vital. It's simply got to be done!'

'Then hadn't you better stick around and look after that yo'self, m'man?' Jockey Dunn inquired.

'No.'

'Aw, let Dave Harper go!' Dunn advised. 'He ain't wuth a bucket o' hot spit!'

'I'm going to get him!' Roscoe raved.

'Well, George, I ain't so shuah I know where Buffalo Valley is,' Dunn said. 'These is furrin parts to me.'

'Me, too,' Bowes said.

'Boys, you've got your consarned orders!' Roscoe declared dangerously. 'Carry 'em out, blast you, or stand and answer to me right now!'

'This ain't the Army, George,' Dunn began. 'You can't go gallivantin'—'

'I can too, Jockey!' Roscoe retorted, his anger abruptly cold and the more deadly because of it. 'Do as you're told—or I'll draw on you!'

'As to that,' Dunn announced, 'I've faced a heap worse. But where in tarnation's the sense of men in trouble startin' to bite at each other's backsides? I'll shoot that feller Jardin, and the little woman too—though I'm minded to take my pleasure of her first. That's if so be she's still around to be killed. We done left her on her ownsome, and I figure she'd have took that as an invitation to bolt.'

'Petticoats and all!' Roscoe sneered. 'She can't have got far. She hasn't come this way, so she must be afoot. Her horse is standing in the corral outside Harper's stables. That's where I'm going right now after my own!'

'Awright!' Dunn sighed. 'We'll 'tend to the dirty work. But you get back good and soon, George. Our bunch are sort of middlin' cowhands and such. They ain't exactly the cream o' North and South, and they shuah do need to be properly led. Yes, suh! 'Specially to that there Buffler Valley.'

'Get this through your thick skull, Jockey!' Roscoe commanded nastily. 'Buffalo Valley will keep—once Jardin and the Carter woman are dead. You can depend on me, so make sure I can depend on you. I should be back before dusk. We'll ride into that valley latish and hit the farm by moonlight. How does that sound?'

'You're the man,' Dunn allowed submissively.

Roscoe jerked his chin emphatically. Then off he went to his right, running fast, and the watching Jardin imagined that he would be heading for the household stables, which he believed he had seen opposite the Harper dwelling and at the edge of the northern half of the ranch site.

'He won't be back,' Olly Bowes averred. 'What's he think? That rancher won't be dawdling. He knows how many beans make five. You don't get a place like this by bein' a deadbeat.'

'I don't know for that,' Jockey Dunn said shortly. 'Let's go into the barn and finish Jardin off. We can look for Mrs Carter once he's dead.'

'What's the hurry?' Bowes disapproved balkily. 'Jardin will keep a bit longer. Let's find the woman first.'

'No,' Dunn said, walking slowly into the barn now, chin turned across his shoulders. 'All of a sudden I don't feel comfortable about that sidewinder. Dunno why.'

'Son, you're gittin' to be a real old woman, that's your trouble!' Bowes declared sourly.

Dunn made a rude gesture at his comrade, then turned his face to the front. Jardin watched the man quicken his step and come deep into the barn, a slight wariness in the tilt of his head. He seemed unquestionably to have picked up an intuitive warning that there could be some form of unexpected danger present from the captive whom his companion and he had left so helplessly bound before going for their meal. As Dunn began to round the pile of firewood, his tread checked perceptibly and his hand went to his gun.

Stiffening in response, Jardin gripped his big axe with both hands. He hoped to be able to use the tool as a club and floor the dog-headed villain with a blow from the back of the bit. But Dunn evidently detected something of his figure in the gloom ahead, for he let out a hissing gasp of disbelief—which seemed to contradict the doubt that he had already expressed—and whipped out his revolver, the weapon flashing instantly in Jardin's direction.

Jardin heard the whimper of the bullet in his left ear, and realized instantly that there could be neither hesitation nor mercy in his retaliation; so he hurled his axe at Dunn with all his strength; and Jockey, his pupils still shrunk to the greater light outside, could only strain at the shadow of the movement and duck instinctively when it was already too late to avoid the missile. He dipped his head straight into the path of the whirling tool, and the cutting edge of its heavy blade struck him full at the centre of his forehead, literally splitting his skull like a log; and he fell, a fountain of blood rising from his wound, threshed violently for a moment or two upon the floor, then tossed over onto his back and lay still.

'Hey—Jockey!' Olly Bowes called uncertainly from the barn's threshold. 'You all right?'

Well forward of the heaped firewood now, Jardin saw Bowes pull his sixgun and begin advancing into the barn—more in response to the noise of Dunn's fall than anything he could have seen of it—and, perceiving himself to be once more at mortal risk, Jardin lunged for the spot where Jockey lay and snatched up the Colt which rested at the man's side. Bowes clearly detected the movement immediately, interpreted it accurately, and opened fire on Jardin, getting off three shots in little more than a second.

Twice narrowly missed, Jardin answered in the same rapid fashion—evidently getting close himself—for Bowes sprang round instantly and scuttled out of the barn, his shape cutting a black semi-arc through the sunrays as he doubled left and vanished from Jardin's sight where the front wall of the building intervened. Remembering that Bowes and Jockey had dismounted and left their horses standing somewhere close to the entrance of the barn, Jardin gave instant chase, hurling himself into a run, but he reached the exit only in time to see that Bowes had already mounted up and was fleeing at the gallop from the spot not six yards away where Dunn's horse was still available. Coming to, Jardin extended his arm and triggered the remaining contents of his cylinder at the fugitive, but he still failed to score a hit and Bowes went on threshing ahead and was virtually out of gunshot before Jardin could spin out and cram a round or two of fresh ammunition into the exposed chambers of his appropriated six-shooter.

Cursing himself for the misses, Jardin paused to make a full reload from his belt and watch the horseman receding to the northwest of the ranch site. He guessed where Bowes would be going. The man would be returning to the prairie hollow where the Tupper herd was being held. The question was what precisely he would do when he got there. Jardin didn't see the man as a natural leader, but you could never be certain about any fellow's capabilities in an emergency—and Bowes was old enough to be very experienced.

Knowing that Roscoe had left to hunt down Dave Harper—and that it was vital to the badmen that both Jim Lyons, the Texas trailherder lying wounded in Buffalo Valley, and the escaped Jardin should still be killed—Bowes could well have the wit to work out that Jardin would not journey to town first and enlist the aid of the law but ride to Buffalo Valley instead—in order to warn the people at home of the possibly impending danger from the Roscoe gang—and thus place himself in the position where his enemies could kill two birds with one stone. Or three, perhaps, since any thinking man in Bowes's place must realize that Jardin would do everything in his power to find Adah Carter and take her home with him before she could get into further difficulties on the Box H. It was, perhaps, a slightly complicated situation—but only in its exposition—and Jardin saw the practical steps needed to meet it as direct and easy enough. Thus it was largely a matter of action now.

Holstering his appropriated sixgun, Jardin ran to Jockey Dunn's horse and sprang into the saddle. Applying the rowels, he rode a short distance northwards, then made a right turn across the front of the ranch house and peered in at the windows as he cantered by, hoping to glimpse Adah Carter if she were still in the dwelling; but in fact he favoured Dunn's notion that the terrified woman would have seized her chance, when Roscoe and the other two villains present had left her alone on suspecting that Dave Harper had decamped on the late sheriff's well-placed horse, and fled into the land. It figured that she would be heading eastwards right now, since she too would realize that her home in Buffalo Valley was much nearer than the town of Standish—even if it did offer a lot less in the way of safety.

Accepting it as a gamble, with the odds well in his favour, Jardin put the Box H ranch house behind him and drew his mount's head a few degrees to the left, moving now on the line down which he believed Adah Carter would have set out for home, and he hadn't covered more than a mile when he saw the woman stumbling across the range, her skirts lifted and boot-heels frequently toppling her a little from one gopher hole to the next. Spurring at Jockey Dunn's red gelding, a very good nag, he soon bore down on the fleeing woman, and it pleased him to see the expression of fear that she swung on him, when first she heard his horse, turn to one of relief as she recognised him. Then he drew to a virtual halt beside her and, smiling, lifted her off the ground with his left arm and swung her onto the saddle in front of him. 'You all right?' he asked.

'Are we going home, Ben?'

'That's right.'

'Will they,' she gulped breathlessly—'will they follow us?'

'Daresay.'

'Won't that mean a fight?'

'A big one, if I've got it pegged right,' Jardin replied, gazing northwestwards across the range towards the position of that sunken place where the Tupper herd was confined as he stirred up the horse beneath them and set it running strongly again in the general direction of Buffalo Valley.

'Frank's the only man on our farm now Sam is buried in the plot out the back.'

'Don't let that fret you,' Jardin said, trying to comfort her with his calmness. 'There's Harry and Joe and me on our place, and likely a young guy named Jim Lyons too—one of *the* fighting breed. That Texas crowd, I mean. Nor should you underestimate your sister-in-law. Rosemary is one of the best shots I've ever run across, and she's got as much courage as any man was ever given. You might surprise yourself, too, if you were forced to pick up a Winchester and start shooting. Regarding the numbers involved— As I see it, the Jardins and the Carters are in the same mess here, so they might as well stand together at our place.'

'I don't believe Rosemary will have that,' Adah said demurely.

'Oh, I know what she is,' Jardin said. 'But if you explain to her clearly how things are, I don't believe you'll find she's that stupid. If she is, refer her to me.'

'You're not—'

'I'm not among her favourite guys at the moment?' Jardin queried wryly. 'I upset her a little yesterday morning. Not that she takes much upsetting. We'll have to see about Rosemary. I suspect she needs a little tenderising these days.'

'I'll tell her you said that.'

'Not if you want to get home, you won't!' Jardin laughed. 'Do you want to get home?'

'I've never been so frightened in my life.'

'I was pretty scared myself back there, Adah,' Jardin confessed. 'Takes years off your life!'

The woman shuddered, and it was obvious that she could have said a lot more, but she looked to the front and

Jardin raised the rhythm of the horse another notch, content now just to ride the miles necessary to bring their home valley in sight. Before long it occurred to him that they were now approaching the eastern boundary of the Harper ranch, and he glanced back again—knowing that this was the last chance he would get for the present to gaze across the full panorama of the land on which today's adventures had taken place—and his eyes went again to the approximate position of the sunken cow cache, movement out to the left of it catching his glance and then holding his attention.

Small upon the grass at this distance, a rider was coming in from the west. He was doing a fair lick, and his back was bent forward, but something in the poise of his head identified him for Jardin. The man yonder was George Roscoe. Was it possible that Roscoe could have overtaken Dave Harper, settled with the rancher, and almost made it back to the hiding place of the Tupper herd in the time? Yes, it was possible; but it would have depended on circumstances, of course—and of these there could have been too many to readily consider—yet Jardin could hardly conceive of a sequence so rapid that Roscoe could have achieved all that he set out to do and still got back again less than three-quarters of an hour. No, it was far more probable that the gang-boss had heard the shots fired back at the Box H ranch site, pondered on their meaning for a few minutes, then fetched his horse about in admission of the fact that there were indeed matters behind him of greater importance than overtaking and gunning down a gutless cattleman.

Conscious that Adah Carter was becoming curious as to what was holding his attention in the country behind them, Jardin looked to the front again and steadied his horse over a considerable tract of rough ground that also carried a wide swathe of recent cattle tracks. He reckoned those would have been the marks left by Tom Tupper's herd before the cows bedded down last night; and, gazing to his right, he saw, not so very far away, the high walls and slightly undulating bottom of Blue Grass Valley, with the deep-worn presence of the trail south down its well-watered, bluish-green centre. There was an instant of regretful longing in Jardin as he looked that way, for the town, so easily reached through there, could provide a weight of assistance that would deter any attack; but, if there had ever been a temptation in him before this to turn here and ride through the valley to Standish, it was utterly gone now. With George Roscoe back and leading the badmen again, the attack on Buffalo Valley was a certainty. He and Adah Carter could not get home too quickly with their warning of trouble to come.

Putting the rough behind him, Jardin spurred on eastwards, but the reaching distance seemed to mock and he felt the need to go faster and faster. His horse, however, was only flesh and blood—and double-mounted too—so he had to quell his impatience and ignore the scenes which his imagination produced of what was probably happening back where George Roscoe held sway. Roscoe would not seek opinions or waste words. He would say what went and nothing more. Then he would give the sign for his men to leave the cattle-filled hollow and gallop eastwards. They could be on their way at this very moment, and a lead of four or five miles would soon dwindle before unencumbered riders pushing hard.

Jardin kept his mount going at about three-quarters of its full pace. Steadily and monotonously it stretched and thudded across the plain. The landmarks were few hereabouts, and Jardin barely recognised any that were present. He travelled this ground but seldomly in normal circumstances, and that made the miles seem a good deal longer. But they wore away, as he knew they must if he tackled them in a sensible manner; and, though he took a very careful look back as the northern end of Buffalo Valley drew on, he saw no sign of the badmen upon the land in his wake and reckoned that he and the woman seated before him had maintained the greater part of whatever their initial lead over George Roscoe and his gang had been up to now.

Their journey still free of incident, Jardin and his companion entered Buffalo Valley and travelled southwards down its length. After another sweaty, patience-fraying spell, they came to the Jardin farm and halted. Here Jardin sprang out of his saddle and, standing with his hands upon his mount's side—while Adah Carter lifted herself back into the seat which he had just left—he said: 'Ride over to your own place—pronto! Get your people over here. Don't listen to their ifs and buts. This is life and death. It really, truly is! Get it through to them with all your force—and get them over here!'

The woman stared down at him, seeming dispossessed by the intensity of his expression..

'Right?' he demanded.

She nodded, then off she went, galloping

across the valley floor in the direction of the Carter farm buildings.

Jardin turned to face his own house. He ran towards the front door. This opened in his path. Through the doorway he went and into the living room, where he saw his sister Emma standing at the end of the table, while the slim and big-boned shape of the young Texan, Jim Lyons, was in process of raising up in an armchair beside the fireplace. 'Whatever's up?' Emma asked, paling. 'You look like you've got the Nations at your heels!'

'I have the next best thing,' he said. 'Name of George Roscoe.' He went on to swiftly explain all about Roscoe and the day's doings over on the Box H, stressing that, in order that the evil parties might avoid immediate retribution and hang on to their ill-gotten gains, the three people now present in Buffalo Valley who could bear witness against them had to die—Jim Lyons, Adah Carter, and himself. 'At that, sis,' he added, 'you saved my bacon this morning by going to the law in town. If poor Sheriff Holst hadn't showed up on the Box H when he did—full of the right accusations—I'd never have got this far today.'

'Sounds like I'm the cause of the trouble,' Jim Lyons observed weakly. 'If you'd just rode past when you saw me out yonder—'

'Fiddlesticks!' Emma cut in hotly. 'My big brother had already got his teeth into something, and he can't stay out of trouble to save his life!' She paused to cast the young man a reassuring smile. 'You're not to blame for anything, Jim. All the guilt is elsewhere. There seem to be some very wicked folk around. You were just a cowboy doing his job when the shooting started.' Now she wagged a chiding finger. 'All I have against you is that you won't obey orders. You should be in bed!'

'I did go to bed,' Lyons said defensively. 'I got up again, that's all.'

'He's a Texan,' Jardin explained. 'There's no fun being in bed.'

'Fun!' Emma almost screamed.

'They do say the Good Lord takes the

thought for the deed,' Lyons commented mournfully—'and I sure as hell left home looking for fun.'

'We've got another lunatic in the house!' Emma declared.

'It's no good talking to women, boy!' Jardin sympathised. 'They simply don't understand men! That's the cross we fellers have to bear!'

'You haven't the sense of a newborn baby between the lot of you!' Emma announced, fairly dancing. 'It sounds like we're about to get the house shot up—if nothing worse—and you speak of fun, Ben!'

'It doesn't really matter a damn what I speak of, sis,' Jardin said shortly. 'Nothing changes what we have to do.' Drawing his six-shooter, he eased back the weapon's hammer and spun its cylinder. 'We have to stand off George Roscoe and his apes. If we fail, everybody will be slain. Of that, little sister, you may be sure.'

'And the Carters are coming over here?'

'I'm praying so.'

'Then I'd better go outside and call

brothers Joe and Harry in,' the girl observed.

'You better had, Emma,' Jardin agreed. 'When you've done that, take Alma and Rita, our sister-in-laws, into the pantry. You'll have the safety of plenty of walls around you then.'

Emma nodded, then went running out through the back of the house.

'You better go with 'em, boy,' Jardin encouraged, hooking a thumb in the pantry's direction.

'Twice!' Lyons snorted, easing himself over to the left so that he could get at his holster. 'You know, Ben, that sister of yours is all right.'

'Stick around,' Jardin invited, tongue in cheek. 'She'll look better yet.'

Then he went outside and looked across the valley to the Carter place. He saw at once that Adah had moved fast and plainly done what had been asked of her in a fully convincing fashion; for he could already see the Carters leaving their farm and making for the Jardin land. Adah was again riding Jockey Dunn's horse, and now her children were clinging around her body, while Rosemary was seated on her own mount and had her brother Frank running along behind her, his right hand holding the brute's tail. Jardin saw guns present too, and he didn't doubt the will of the people over there to use them.

Despite their extreme haste, it took a few minutes for the Carters to cross the mile or more of the valley floor, and Jardin watched uneasily throughout—his gaze flicking northwards up the valley in an ever-growing fear of the worst—but the crossing was completed without disaster bearing down on them, and Rosemary Carter and her brother Frank lifted down the children from Adah's horse and went into the house. Jardin stepped up to assist Adah out of the saddle, but she raised a staying hand in that moment and said tautly: 'I see them, Ben! They're coming fast! They'll be here in a minute!'

'Good,' Jardin said quietly, picking out the oncoming riders as he helped her to the ground. 'The sooner the better.'

He meant exactly that.

TEN

Jardin had given his battle orders and helped Jim Lyons over to the front window, where it had been agreed that the pair should defend the eastern face of the house, while the other three men—Joe and Harry Jardin, and Frank Carter—had taken themselves off to defend the rest of the dwelling from other windows about the place. Rosemary Carter, her Winchester cocked and ready, had gone to the pantry to take shelter with the other women, but Jardin had no doubt that the dark woman would be out of there and shooting with the men when the need became urgent.

Standing at the right-hand edge of the window, Jardin slanted his gaze up the valley and waited for the oncoming horsemen—who were already fully visible to him—to halt outside, and this they did about three minutes after the Jardin front

218

door had been locked against them and the retaining bar set in place. Having already commanded that fire should be held until the other side started shooting, Jardin now watched uncertainly—for no gun had yet been drawn among the badmen—and he wondered what was coming next, since George Roscoe was looking grave rather than murderous and somehow gave the impression that he would like to avoid a fight. 'Ben!' he suddenly shouted. 'Ben, I know you're in there and can hear me!'

'What do you want, George?'

'We saw those people joining you from across the valley.'

'Figures. So?'

'No need for all your folk to—'

'Cut it out!' Jardin interrupted. 'What you want is for me, this Texas boy—and Adah Carter—to step outside the door and take our medicine. Forget it, George!'

'Ben, I'm trying my hardest to make this as easy as possible for all concerned.'

'You're a liar, mister!' Jardin retorted flatly. 'You are out to nail some of us the easy way. Then kill the rest when they've turned their backs. They're all witnesses now.'

'You should trust me, Ben.'

'I can't. There's no way. You're the same scheming devil you were in the bivouac.'

'Well, there!' Roscoe sighed. 'I must kill you and that Texas boy, but Adah Carter is just another hysterical female. The rest of them don't know honeydew from a cowpat. We can bluff our way past anything they say. It ain't believable, you see? So how do you answer me then? Are you and that Texan going to come out here and take it like brave men?'

'You'll kill them all, George,' Jardin retorted. 'You've got to!'

'No—'

'Let's have no more of this damned nonsense!' Jardin roared. 'Either go away —or start what you came for!'

'You're going to regret this, Ben,' Roscoe said, pulling his revolver.

'Not half as much as you are!' Jardin promised, shrinking back and jerking his own weapon as a deft and acutely angled shot from Roscoe shattered the windowpane and passed within inches of his chest.

Squaring to his work, Jardin fired back, trying to kill Roscoe before the battle could get started, but his bullet did no more than clip the front of the man's saddle, and lead spat through the window from the other guns outside before he could get a second shot in. Covered in fragments of windowframe and splinters of glass, Jardin knelt down under the sill, joining Jim Lyons, who was already blazing away quite fearlessly in reply to the fusillade from without, and the pair of them knocked down two of the enemy and badly wounded a third—who hinged over and went wheeling out of the fight, clearly finished—with their first few shots.

The riders outside began to shout for the sake of it, both in fear and defiance, and they started to back and swing their horses, seeking to put distance between themselves and the defending guns at the front window. This was less than advantageous to the pistol-shooting

Jardin and Jim Lyons—for their Colts were essentially short range weapons—but then the sharper crack of a rifle joined the booming of the revolvers and Jardin looked up and round and saw that Rosemary Carter had joined them in shooting at the badmen from a sitting position on the end of the table. Jardin's recent praise of her marksmanship was instantly vindicated when one of the riders beyond the farmhouse went end-over-tip out of his saddle and landed on the grass in a writhing heap. 'Nicely!' Jardin applauded. 'I can't see that bunch taking too much of this!'

'They won't give up that easily,' Rosemary Carter returned, hardly blinking as a bullet whizzed in through the window and literally clipped a lock from her hair.

'You won't be here to see whether they do or not,' Jardin breathed. 'For heaven's sake get down here, Rosemary! That was too close!'

But Rosemary Carter simply raised her Winchester again, briefly followed a new target with the end of her gun barrel, and squeezed off, emptying another saddle. 'That takes care of him!' she announced grimly. 'Two can play at that game.'

'Since you have the stomach for shooting men,' Jardin encouraged, 'do us all a favour and knock George Roscoe over. He's the fellow with the bruised up face who sits tall and shouts a lot.'

'I know who he is,' the dark woman said. 'I got a peep at him just now when he was talking to you. I've been trying to get a clear shot at him, but he's a crafty one and keeps putting other riders between him and my rifle.'

'George Roscoe is nobody's hero,' Jardin affirmed, 'but crafty he is. What's the varmint up to now? Those fools are never going to risk charging us!'

'They are,' Jim Lyons said. 'That's exactly what they aim to do!'

'But that's a hell of a thin line they've drawn,' Jardin observed. 'I wish I could make out what Roscoe is saying to them.'

'They're only six,' Lyons counted. 'They ain't enough, Ben. They're beat if they try it that way!'

'I'm inclined to agree with you, boy,' Jardin said, cocking his revolver as the fairly distant horsemen began their charge. 'It's a pity George hasn't got sense enough to see it!'

'I'm not sure they're bent on what you think,' Rosemary Carter said.

'How's that?'

'I think they want to get into your farm buildings,' Rosemary explained, 'and shoot at the house from the windows in their walls.'

'Yeah, it could be that,' Jardin said, frowning. 'I belittle Roscoe, yes, but he does know what he's doing as a rule. The day's getting through. Maybe he plans on a stand-off until tonight. If they can get into the buildings, they should be able to lie low now and then creep up on the house after dark. Crafty!'

They were firing again now, but the riders thundering towards them had learned their lesson by this time and were keeping low on the necks of their mounts. They were also drifting across the face of the building, which made individuals more difficult to aim at in the immediate sense and carried them completely wide of the defenders' arc of fire in the longer one. This enabled them—as Jardin soon heard clearly—to swing their galloping mounts round the southern end of the house and then turn northwards into the second half of a circular movement which also appeared to reveal another part of their strategy. 'I think they want to find out how many guns we've got in here,' Jardin said, shaking fuming shells from his cylinder and replacing them with new cartridges—'and where they're placed.'

Then, quite unexpectedly, a shudder passed through the house. It seemed to have been caused by an impact at the dwelling's rear northern corner. 'Ben!' Emma Jardin called from the pantry. 'Did you hear that? I believe somebody just rode into that beam which juts from the back corner of the house opposite the stables!'

Jardin had had the same impression himself. He and his brothers had always realized how dangerous that extra beam was—built into the upper house a few years ago to shore up cyclone damage—but they had deliberately left its jutting end unshortened for fear that the heavy sawing necessary to making a neater job of things might weaken the work over all. Fully aware that the piece of timber was there when they were moving around the exterior of the house—and conscious, too, that it was too high for anybody to walk into—the men had been content to accept the slight risk that an unwary horseman might ride into it some day; but, obeying that age-old law which has it that anything which can happen in a given situation finally will, it seemed that a rider must have just gone full-butt into the beam and perhaps done himself mortal damage. Not that it mattered a scrap in the present circumstances, of course—for the attackers were blessedly reduced by any means at all—but Jardin did have the feeling that, when considering the lead position in the circling movement, it could well have been Roscoe who had brought himself down thus. Certainly the confused shouting among the riders outside suggested that something of the kind had occurred.

Rising abruptly, Jardin covered his action with a quick: 'Going to take a look!' Then he hurled out of the living room and into the rear of the house, where he just as swiftly drew the bolts of the back door and lifted the retaining bar out of its slots, setting it aside.

Opening the door, he thrust his head out—taking his chance on a bullet—and, looking to his right, saw a horse standing riderless to one side and a shape that was undoubtedly George Roscoe lying sprawled beneath the two-feet six inches of beam that thrust out of a vent high up on the corner of the building there. Then movement beyond the downed figure drew his attention, and he saw a man whom he instantly recognised as Olly Bowes heading for Roscoe on foot. Bowes held a six-shooter in his right hand, and he fired at Jardin as their eyes met; but haste was perhaps his undoing, for the bullet did no more than whisk his enemy's hair. This prompted Jardin to shoot back along the line of the gunflash opposite, and scarlet immediately splashed into the front of Bowes's shirt. The badman fell onto his back, legs spread apart and arms similarly positioned. There was no further movement from him, and Jardin knew there never would be. Bowes had been hit in the heart, and no man could survive that kind of wound.

Moving at a crouched run, Jardin went now to where George Roscoe lay. Kneeling beside the ashen-faced man, he first glanced up and across the open ground between the house and the buildings on his left, seeking to ascertain what had become of the surviving horsemen from the attacking gang, and he saw them riding off the farm and northwards up the valley at top speed. Two of the men were craning, and Jardin emptied his gun at them—more to emphasize his feelings of good riddance than anything else—and, though he failed to score any more hits, he knew for certain within himself that the badmen would not be coming back. They had achieved nothing here and already paid a heavy price in blood and death; and even if they still possessed the will—which he believed unlikely—it was clear that they were no longer in sufficient numbers to control the Texas herd for which they had killed Tom Tupper and company that morning. It was not too much to say that they had done it all for nothing—and that they might eventually hang for the same.

Putting up his gun, Jardin began his examination of the felled Roscoe. It was at once evident that the man's neck was broken. Impacted vertebrae were visible under the skin of his nape, and the pale fluid seeping out of his ears suggested that he had also fractured his skull when he had ridden around the corner of the house and driven the top of his head against the beam that jutted there. He appeared to have died instantly and, though either injury would have killed him, that could have been more than he deserved. Anyway, it seemed to be all over, and Jardin stood up feeling a kind of relief that somehow fell short of elation. But he supposed he had been in the wars these last three days, and a man only had it in him to feel just so much at the peak of his emotional force. After that, the edge was dulled and he simply accepted what came—for good or ill. Yet—there ought to be more joy in him than this.

Midnight had long since struck on the grandfather clock downstairs, but still Jardin could not sleep.

There had been a lot of friendly talk earlier between his family and the Carters. Port wine and good whisky had been drunk, and angel cake and brandy snaps eaten. There had been a feeling of thanksgiving and triumph in the air, and everything had ended in kisses and a spontaneous pumping of hands. The feud was as dead as those villains lying under the old tarpaulin out in the shed, and there had been laughter—and tears—over the absurdity of what had happened back in Tennessee. It was going to be a good future. A lot of sense had been talked. They had put away that idea of 'tolling the Texans,' and declared their intention of using joint labour. He, Ben, was going across to the Carter farm to work with Frank—who had humbly admitted that he alone could not run the place—and he had nudged Rosemary into hinting that she might marry him before long. That had fairly brought the roof down, and it seemed that there could never be sorrow or despair in Buffalo Valley again. Yet still he could not rest on this auspicious night.

That earlier sense of flatness persisted. Somehow it had not come out right—all had ended too tamely. Though he imagined that tame would be the wrong word for it when he began trying to explain to the law the chain of events which had ended with the battle on his farm. Oh, yes! He had some cause for worry. Yet his mood went beyond that. There was no real end to what had happened; everything was simply petering out. But that was ridiculous, of course. The feud was over, George Roscoe was dead, and all the dirty doings planned on the Box H had finished. What more could be expect—or want?

His bed was uncomfortable; feathers

were too hot for this time of the year. He rolled over, sweating. Outside his window the moonlight hung like a shroud. There was no wind in the valley tonight; everything was utterly still. The grass had no voice, and the silence crept. A man could feel the tension within the firmament. This hour might be hurtling towards starset. Yet nothing moved.

Then he seemed to hear a footfall outside the house. The sound was the more audible because he knew it could not be there. He felt a presence under his window. He had the impression of a face turned upwards and looking at it. Was it the ghost of a man newly dead on its first outing? What nonsense! But Jardin's flesh crept nevertheless, and suddenly he got out of bed and stood there stiffly, listening. Fainter than ever, that perhaps insubstantial boot stirred again. He shook himself. He wasn't imagining things; it was almost beyond him to do that. He was a watcher by night, and a man born to the silent earth: a part wild thing that was totally aware. If he

232

had detected somebody outside, then that person was indeed there.

Snatching his trousers off the chair beside his bed, he pulled them on. Then he drew his Colt from the gunbelt which he had draped over the headrail of his bed and thrust it into his waistband. After that he walked to the window and eased it up its runners as silently as he could, pushing his head out into the moonlight beyond and looking down, eyes sweeping rapidly from the left to right and back again. Nobody. Yet it seemed to him that he could hear the faintest of hissing noises and just detect an acrid smell in the still air.

For a long moment he pondered stupidly, having perhaps been nearer to sleep than he had supposed, and then he realized what the odour was and galvanised as to the zip of an inner lightning. Without a thought for the risk to his back or limbs, he swung a leg over the sill, ducked his upper body after it, then brought the second leg up and over to join the first. For a split second he sat there on the window ledge, then launched himself into space, and down he plunged for about fifteen feet, his bare soles hitting the ground a shuddering smack and his weight throwing him forward onto his face.

Badly jarred, but otherwise unharmed, he scrambled to his feet and stood looking around him shakily. Once again his ears strained, and he heard a sudden movement from the southern end of the house. Somebody was running away from the wall there, and it was obvious that they had been up to no good. In fact he was now convinced as to the kind of mischief on which they had been engaged.

Terror filled him. His mind and body threatened to freeze up. He didn't know which way to turn. Yet, reasoning dimly from the fact that the last piece of audible movement had reached him from the right—which suggested to his over-heating imagination that that was the direction he need worry about least for a short spell—he went running to his left and rounded the corner at which George Roscoe had died, seeing before him and at the foot of the wall adjacent, a fiery tendril that was spraying tiny sparks into the gloom and giving a full measure of the stench which had first tickled his nostrils after he had opened the window of his bedroom.

Dynamite! Heavens but he had smelled enough of the stuff at the Crippled Indian! The wall had been mined!

Still with no thought for other than what must be done to survive, Jardin fell to his knees beside the spluttering fuse and picked up the mine itself—which consisted of four sticks of dynamite bound together with twine—and then plucked out the fuse about three inches short of detonation point. After that, supposing that his arrival outside had recently disturbed the placement of another bundle like this one on the further side of the house, he dropped the now harmless mine and, leaping erect once more, doubled back and raced around the building until he came upon the second dynamite charge which he judged to have been set to balance the first.

With every nerve and muscle now reacting to his mind at maximum speed,

Jardin sank down and did as before, plucking out the fuse which had been fired to detonate the dynamite within seconds of that moment and casting it well clear. Then he dropped the mine itself between his knees and turned his eyes upwards in relief. Yet he was instantly forced to realize that his silent prayer of thanks was premature, for he glimpsed the faintest of red glows fanning beyond the front corner of the house on his right.

An involuntary shout of horror burst from his lips. Once more he leapt to his feet and started running. For he had just perceived what had happened and where he had made his latest mistake. Four mines had been intended, one for each wall of the farmhouse, but only three had actually been set—the fourth having been foregone, perhaps because the enemy had heard or otherwise sensed something of Jardin's wakeful presence in the bedroom at the back of the house.

Jardin dived around the angle which seemed to rush at him. Now he lurched and blundered along the face of the dwelling, heading for the front door—not far from which he could see the third mine sparking—then, first cutting a foot and similarly injuring a knee as he dropped beside the last bundle of dynamite, he seized the mine in the same fashion as the other two and made to yank the fuse from its tamping, but he realized in the same particle of time that it had burned too low to remove from the explosives. The whole lot was going to blow up before he could draw another breath!

Doing the only thing he could, Jardin threw himself backwards, landing hard on his shoulder-blades, and he used the force of his arrival thus to increase the strength of his arms as he flung the mine over his face and away from him. The sheer desperation of his effort sent it arcing for perhaps thirty yards, and it rent apart just before it touched the ground again. The explosion was a massive one, and it blew the windows of the house inwards and uprooted the tiles as the remaining blast swept over the rooftop like a brief but hugely destructive gale.

Ears ringing, Jardin struggled into a sitting position as quickly as he could and found it difficult to credit when he saw the shape of a big man charging towards him from the left. The other held a revolver and was firing at him time after time. Reacting instinctively, Jardin pulled the six-shooter from his own waistband and fired back, answering shot for shot at the same rapid speed as his enemy was shooting. He felt his trousers plucked twice and his right forearm burned once, but it was his fire that told, for his attacker—and undoubtedly the man who had tried to blow up the house—staggered suddenly and fell, his pistol spilling just visibly from his grasp and landing beside him.

Rising, Jardin closed on his fallen enemy—ready to shoot again if he had to—but the other lay there gasping the unfulfilling breaths of one close to the end. 'Why did you come back, Harper?' Jardin demanded, more incensed by the fact of the rancher's return than its actual significance. 'Dammit, you were clear and away! Only life matters, man!'

'I—I couldn't give it all up,' the dying man muttered. 'I built—built it, Jardin. Knew—knew Roscoe would follow. Was—was laying for him, blast it, but—but—'

'Sure, he turned round and came back this way to kill off us witnesses,' Jardin supplied, 'and it figures you made up your mind to do the job yourself when George made a mess of it.'

Harper said nothing more. It was plain that he had just died. Jardin sat down heavily beside the body. He wondered how long it would be before his frantically yelling family came out of the house to give him a hand here. There was one more body to lay with the rest.

Now it was over. Even beyond the shadows of the night the future wore the glory of the dawn.

This Large Print Book for the Partially sighted, who cannot read normal print, is published under the auspices of

THE ULVERSCROFT FOUNDATION

THE ULVERSCROFT FOUNDATION

. . . we hope that you have enjoyed this Large Print Book. Please think for a moment about those people who have worse eyesight problems than you . . . and are unable to even read or enjoy Large Print, without great difficulty.

You can help them by sending a donation, large or small to:

The Ulverscroft Foundation, 1, The Green, Bradgate Road, Anstey, Leicestershire, LE7 7FU, England.

or request a copy of our brochure for more details.

The Foundation will use all your help to assist those people who are handicapped by various sight problems and need special attention.

Thank you very much for your help.